Real Mermaids
DON'T NEED HIGH HEELS

To
Next
book is
in Feb.
will
arrive
then.
Love
Santa

HÉLÈNE BOUDREAU

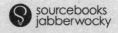

sourcebooks
jabberwocky

Published by Sourcebooks Jabberwocky, an imprint of Sourcebooks, Inc.
P.O. Box 4410, Naperville, Illinois 60567-4410
(630) 961-3900
Fax: (630) 961-2168
www.jabberwockykids.com

Library of Congress Cataloging-in-Publication data is on file with the publisher.

Source of Production: Webcom, Toronto, Ontario, Canada
Date of Production: May 2013
Run Number: 20530

Printed and bound in Canada.

WC 10 9 8 7 6 5 4 3 2

For Charlotte,
who is one of my first (and fastest!) readers

Chapter One

NINTH GRADE. THE BEGINNING of high school!
To say I was excited, walking up the steps of Port
Toulouse Regional High, would be a *bit* of an understatement.

Finally, I'd graduated from junior high's mind-numbing
field trips, soggy pizza Fridays, and lame school rules, and
I'd moved on to the free periods, off-campus lunch privileges, and freedom of high school. Yay!

Sure, our small seaside town of Port Toulouse didn't
actually have enough people for separate elementary,
junior high, and high schools. So technically I was entering
the same gray concrete building I'd been going to since
kindergarten, but still.

Now that I was in *ninth* grade, I got to enter the school
through the big blue door on the far side of the parking lot
next to the regional library. Oh, and the community rec center.

We Port Toulousians liked to get the most out of our
public buildings.

"You ready, Fish Girl?" my best friend, Cori, whispered
as we paused at the top of the school steps, about to go

inside. She was "dressed for success" in a cool *Cori Original* outfit she'd designed over the summer—a flowy, sleeveless teal top over batik-dyed jeans. I think a tenth-grade girl actually gasped in admiration as we passed.

"*So* ready," I replied, adjusting my backpack over my shoulder.

And it was true. I'd just spent the past four months trying to rescue my mermaid mother from a bunch of mer criminals who were keeping her captive in our nearby lake. I freed her from there to the ocean, lost her again, then finally found her in a tidal pool behind Port Toulouse Mall (losing my mer-crush Luke in the process). Then, I had to battle Chamberlain Construction and City Hall *and* the Mermish Council to get my mom and Luke back on dry land once and for all.

Now that Mom and Luke were safely back home and on their own two feet, I was *really* ready for things to get back to normal.

Well, as normal as things could get for a part-time mer-girl like me.

"Oh, and you've got to quit it with the Fish Girl stuff," I whispered to Cori, looking around the school yard to see if anyone had glanced our way. "What if someone hears?"

Thankfully, everyone hanging around by the high-school doors was busy texting, talking, or bopping along to something in their earbuds. There were no teachers in orange vests yelling through bullhorns for everyone to get in line, or flags on the school-yard fence to alert everyone whether this was a "pavement" or a "playground" recess depending on how much mud had collected below the slides.

High school = perfection.

"I could call you Fin Face instead, if you really want me to," Cori said cheerily as she swung open the big blue door and we took our first legitimate steps into the legendary halls of Port Toulouse Regional High.

"How about just Jade?" I asked, as we walked by the hallways leading to the town library and rec center and arrived at the windowed high-school office where Ms. Wilma wheeled around in her secretary office chair from her telephone, to the file cabinet, to the teachers' mail slots like a well-oiled bumper car.

"Okay, 'Just Jade,'" Cori smirked, "but pick up the pace or there won't be any good lockers left."

Another perk of high school? Actual lockers! With doors! A far cry from the open-faced cubbyholes we used to have in junior high. But the lockers were first come, first served so that's why we were already in school at 8:30 a.m., even though the first bell wouldn't ring until nine.

We rushed down locker lane by the school gym (again, shared by the community center), which had the only lockers in the school, and snagged a couple of them close to the girls' bathroom. The hallway was already filled with kids yanking on metal doors to make sure their soon-to-be lockers were free of chewing gum and last year's sweaty gym socks.

"These will be perfect." I dialed through the numbers

of the combination lock I'd brought from home and hung it from one of the lockers to claim it. Then I unzipped my backpack and pulled out my brand-spanking-new magnetic mirror, magnetic pen holder, and magnetic white board so I could Pimp My Locker.

"Yeah, and there are two other free ones a few doors down for Luke and Trey." Cori had already taped three hand-drawn *Cori Original* fashion designs to the inside of her locker door and was hanging beads and a hand-dyed scarf from the hook.

"Wow. My locker is so boring compared to yours." I'd thought my magnetic accessories were the best thing since chocolate-covered popcorn back at Office Depot. I'd even gotten them all in glossy black for that tied-together look, but compared to Cori's randomly accessorized locker door, mine looked plain. Sturdy—but plain. Kind of the same way I felt next to Cori, but I'd pretty much gotten used to having a beautiful friend.

"You dork," Cori exclaimed, sketching a quick dress design on my whiteboard with one of my dry-erase markers. It was girly and mermaidy, looking like it belonged on a red carpet. "I'd kill for one of these white boards! Plus, I call first dibs on your mirror after lunch period. I really don't want a replay of that unfortunate spinach incident from last year."

"Okay, okay." I laughed, remembering the afternoon when Cori had looked like a gap-toothed hockey player by the time I caught up with her after lunch and told her she had spinach stuck in her teeth. I scribbled my lock's combination number on a piece of paper and handed it to her. "Guard it with your life."

"Perfect." She took the paper from me and stuffed it in her locker, then scribbled her combination on a paper for me.

"Hey, where are those Martin guys, anyway?" Cori continued, looking around and over the heads in the crowded hallway for Luke and Trey, our…boyfriends. It was still really weird to think of them that way.

"Luke emailed me last night and said their boat's bow line got slashed and the boat drifted from its mooring," I said.

"Wow, really?" Cori asked.

"Yeah," I replied. "And apparently a couple of Jet Skis sank at Talisman Lake Marina, too. They've had to put a security guard on the night shift."

"Why would anyone want to vandalize a bunch of boats?" Cori wondered. "It's just so random."

"I dunno," I said. "But anyway, Luke said they finally found their boat. It had run aground on one of the lake's islands, and judging by the time of the email, I think they were up pretty late. Maybe they just slept in."

"Well, they're going to get stuck with lockers by the water fountain if they don't hurry up." Cori glanced around the hallway.

"Got it covered!" Trey bounced up behind Cori and grabbed her by the shoulders, making her nearly jump out of her skin.

"Hey!" Cori grabbed his hand and turned to give him a peck on the cheek. "I wanted us all to get lockers together."

"We just kept ours from last year," Trey said. "Mine's at the end and Luke's is across from the gym doors."

"Where *is* that little brother of yours?" I glanced over by the gym doors, hoping to catch a glimpse of Luke, but he wasn't there.

"If you mean that guy who just *dominated* at ollies skating over here, look no further." Luke appeared at my side from the other direction, with his skateboard tucked under one arm. He draped his other arm around my shoulder.

My heart did one of those ka-thumpa-thump-thump triple backflips, and a happy feeling spread through me. It had been a few weeks since we'd made our boyfriend-girlfriend status official back at the beach party at Toulouse Point. I still couldn't quite get used to the fact that Luke Martin, mer-boy himself, and I were actually a couple.

An *actual* boyfriend? Me? There was hope for mankind. Um, or mer-kind.

"Yeah, as if. You only wish you were half as good as I am." Trey jabbed his brother in the arm and whispered. "You're forgetting—I'm the land-dwelling kid in the family. Skateboarding is kinda my thing."

The coolest thing was that Luke and I didn't have to hide our mer secret from Trey and Cori. That came in really handy when we'd needed their help with our recent mer-scapades. But like Dad had warned me, the rest of the world couldn't be trusted. If our secret ever got out, who knew what could happen to us?

"Whatever, Bro." Luke rolled his eyes and turned to us. "So, you guys know where you're going?"

"Yeah…I think so." Cori looked down at the class schedule we'd downloaded from the school website the week before. "But they don't have our homerooms on here."

"Where do we find that out?" I asked, sneaking a glance at Luke. His summer tan made his adorable, curvy-lipped smile even brighter, and the sun had highlighted his curly hair to a golden streaked brown. Whoa, he was cute.

Luke caught me looking and blushed.

"There's a list by the front office." Trey nodded in that general direction. "Come on, newbies. We'll show you."

"Newbies?" Cori smirked, slinging her backpack over her shoulder. "You're just lucky we're finally in high school to add a little class to this joint."

"I'm putting you in charge of 'classing up the joint.'" I shut my locker door and attached the combination lock while Luke stashed his skateboard in his locker further down the hallway. "I'm happy to be your wing girl, though."

"Oh, so Fish Girl is *out* and Wing Girl is *in*, then?" Cori joked. "Is there something you're not telling me?"

"Onward!" I ignored her and headed toward the front office.

The hallways were filled with teenagers laughing, gossiping, and listening to music. I smiled at how different everything was from last year. No one giving each other wedgies or making farting noises with their armpits. Finally, we were in high school—lame-free zone.

Luke caught up with us and squeezed my hand in his, further confirming for me that this was going to be the best school year yet.

"How's the boat?" I asked.

"Some damage to the hull but nothing too serious. Our neighbor's speedboat got swamped, though. His whole electronic system is shot."

"Wow, that's rough," I said.

"Yeah, compared to him we got off easy," Luke agreed.

"Other than that, though, how's life?" I asked, though the last time I'd seen him was less than twenty-four hours ago at Cori's while we hung around her pool, enjoying our last hours of summer freedom.

"Good." Luke smiled, then whispered in my ear, sending a shiver through me. "Great."

"Life's about to get ten times better once 'yours truly' passes his driving exam so we don't have to skateboard to school every day," Trey said as he played Angry Birds on his phone. "The commute is killing me."

"You've already failed it twice. Maybe you should actually *study* this time." Luke reached over and flicked a finger over Trey's screen just as we arrived at a crush of people near the school office.

"Hey!" Trey laughed and shrugged off his brother. "You made me go long on that last bird."

A large crowd had gathered around the bulletin

board while everyone tried to find their homerooms. We wormed our way to the front of the group to get a look at the list.

"I've got Miller," Trey said, running his finger down the list to see who else was in his class.

"Harrington," Luke responded.

"Oh, no!" Cori cried. She wriggled her way between Trey and Luke and squinted at the bulletin board. "Jade! We're not in the same class."

She was right. Cori was in Harrington's ninth-tenth grade split class with Luke. The school tended to group grades together for homeroom because of our low student population, but this was the first year since kindergarten Cori and I hadn't been together.

"It's just homeroom," I assured her, trying to hide my disappointment. "We still have some of our actual classes together."

"I guess," Cori said glumly.

Then I noticed something. I had Mrs. Thorne. But Mrs. Thorne was my homeroom teacher from last year. And lo and behold, Mrs. Thorne's class was an eighth-ninth grade split.

"Eighth-ninth? Are you freaking kidding me?" I looked at the list three times to make sure I was reading it correctly. "They've got me in with the junior high kids? Can they do that?"

"Really? Oh, yeah…" Cori narrowed her eyes as if trying to remember something. "Remember? We had homeroom with the seventh graders when we were in sixth. But that was elementary to junior high."

I shook my head. "I've been waiting two whole years to get out of junior high, and now I have to go back there for homeroom? Just great."

"Don't worry." Luke nudged me. "We'll still let you sit with us in the cafeteria."

I turned and leaned heavily against the corridor wall, not believing my bad luck. But Luke was right. If this was the worst that could happen, I wasn't going to let it ruin the perfectly awesome day I was having.

"Hey, Jade, is that your grandma?" Trey let go of Cori's hand and pointed through the glass windows of the school office. Gran had her back turned, talking to Ms. Wilma as she wheeled around in her office chair, ping-ponging from the filing cabinet to the photocopier and back to her desk with a stack of papers.

"What's she doing here?" I wondered aloud and made my way through the crowd to the office doors. Was there something wrong with Mom? Had there been an accident at Dad's work?

"Gran?" I stepped into the office.

Gran turned to me and her round, rosy-cheeked face broke into a sweet, grandmotherly smile. "Oh, hi, Jadie girl. I'm so glad you're here."

I walked over to hug her. "Is everything okay?"

"Oh, yes. Everything is fine," Gran assured me as she rifled through the bingo markers and tissues in her enormous handbag in search of a pen. "I was just about to get Wilma to call you down here on the P.A. I have someone who needs a tour guide."

That's when I noticed a girl about my age standing in front of a map outside the principal's office, clutching a schoolbag like it was a life preserver. It took a few seconds for my mind to register what I was seeing.

Long, golden brown hair, lanky arms and legs, slim shoulders. Last time I'd seen her, she was swimming off into the sunset with her mother and father in Talisman Lake. I touched the friendship bracelet she'd given me, hanging from my wrist.

"Serena?" I whispered and turned to Gran, not quite understanding. "What's *Serena* doing here?"

Chapter Two

M s. WILMA PAPER-CLIPPED A school information package together and handed it to Gran with a smile. "All righty, Mrs. Baxter. You can fill this part out for now, but we'll also need Serena's old school records, immigration information, and proof of residency before we can officially register her."

Register her? My eyes widened, but Gran grasped my arm to shush me before I blurted out our secret in front of Ms. Wilma.

I glanced back at Serena, but she was busy studying a school-district wall map of Port Toulouse and the surrounding areas. Serena stood facing the map, as if entranced by the blue waters against the green land. She traced her finger along the Atlantic Ocean, up our town's canal and across the boat lock that separated the ocean from nearby Talisman Lake, where she'd grown up as a mermaid with her parents, Finalin and Medora, and the rest of the Freshies imprisoned there by the Mermish Council.

Serena's finger stopped at the bridge for a second, then

followed the lake northward through the islands to Dundee where Gran's cottage was. Finally, she traced a path past the cottage to the northernmost part of Talisman Lake a few miles further, where (I hadn't noticed before) the water spilled back into the Atlantic Ocean through a northern passage.

The last time I'd seen Serena, she was a mer-girl in Talisman Lake. In fact, I was the one who'd brought her back there after a trial run on land. Serena's father, Finalin, had not been very happy with me—after all, he'd sacrificed himself to free her from their lake prison in the first place.

But now Serena was back on dry land and registering for high school? *My* high school?

"The school records might take a while because all of the family's worldly possessions were burned in the lava flow, but we'll do what we can," Gran said to Ms. Wilma as she finished scribbling information on Serena's school registration form.

What the heck? Lava flow?

"Serena and her mother are staying with Jade and her dad," Gran continued, "so I'll put that address."

"Oh, that's wonderful," Ms. Wilma said, spinning her chair to look at me. "Jade, it must be nice to have your cousin and aunt stay with you."

"Uh. Yeah," I managed to utter but I wasn't sure I wanted to encourage this latest turn of events.

"Poor thing has been through so much." Gran glanced at Serena and actually *pulled a tissue from her handbag* to dab the corner of her eye. "We just think a bit of routine and structure would do wonders for her, you know?"

Wow, Gran should really audition for the Port Toulouse Theater Company because she was *good*. She snuck a sideways glance at me and winked. Cori, Luke, and Trey waved and pointed at Serena through the office window from the hallway, wondering what was happening. It would help if *I* knew what was happening.

"Of course!" Ms. Wilma exclaimed. "Heaven knows your son's family has had enough tragedy to last a lifetime," she said, alluding to the fact that everyone in Port Toulouse thought my mom had drowned in Talisman Lake the summer before. And now my "aunt" (who was actually Mom with a makeover) and "cousin" Serena's village had been destroyed by a volcanic lava flow? Too bad we hadn't stocked up on life and accident insurance.

"Thank you for understanding," Gran replied, adding a very enthusiastic nose-blow for effect.

"Getting Serena into a new school as soon as possible is probably the best thing for her." Ms. Wilma patted Gran's hand and dropped her voice to a whisper. "I'll do what I can to push this through with Principal Reamer for now. Just try to get the rest of the information to me as soon as you can."

Ms. Wilma filed the registration form in a folder and put it in Principal Reamer's inbox.

"As soon as *humanly* possible," Gran assured her, replacing her pen in her handbag and snapping it shut. "Hey, am I going to see you at bingo on Thursday night? It's winner-take-all, and the jackpot's a big one."

"Wouldn't miss it. Save me a seat," Ms. Wilma replied,

wheeling away toward the coffeemaker on the other side of the office, mug in hand.

Gran went over to Serena and put a hand on her shoulder. Serena jumped, as if being awoken from a trance, then turned and finally noticed I was there.

Jade, Serena rang to me in her mer voice, smiling broadly.

Most people would probably think the ringing sound of Serena's mer voice was actually buzzing from the overhead fluorescent lights because that's what it sounded like to non-mers. I thought mer rings were one of the most annoying sounds on the planet, but that was how all mers communicated.

I still didn't know what on earth was going on, but if Serena was going to be human again, I had to break her mer-speaking habit as quickly as possible.

You need to use your human voice, I rang back and hugged her. *Remember?*

Serena knew the basics of English from what she'd learned from me and Mom last time she was human.

"J-shade…" Serena tried again. Her eyes widened in surprise at the sound of her voice. She turned to Gran and pointed to the map. "Grr-ansh. Water? Mother, Father?"

"Yes, honey," Gran said in a hushed voice. She pointed at the map as if giving a stranger a tour of local landmarks. "This is the bridge we crossed at the canal between the ocean and the lake. And here's the school where we are now, and there is where I live, remember?" She pointed to Dundee on the map, halfway up the lake.

"Thish what?" Serena asked as she pointed to the northernmost part of the lake where it connected to the Atlantic Ocean again.

"That's Folly's Passage," Gran explained. "It connects the lake to the ocean up north, but it's only open during the highest tides of the year. There's actually a famous shipwreck around there from the Second World War called *Fortune's Folly*. The captain missed the tide and ended up capsizing. Divers have been trying to find the ship ever since."

"You mean the canal by the bridge isn't the only way in and out of the lake?" I whispered to Gran, trying to talk quickly so Serena wouldn't catch on.

"Well, Folly's Passage hasn't been used since I was a girl," Gran mumbled back as Serena kept studying the map. "The cliffs have eroded so much from all the forestry people clear-cutting the trees that the passage has filled in, making it pretty shallow. You'd be crazy to take a boat through there now."

I considered this for a second. Most of the Freshie mers hung out by the boat lock at the south end of Talisman Lake where salt water spilled in from the canal. Other than Finalin and Medora, who'd been in the lake the longest, none of the Freshies had made it further north than Dundee because the lake water was too fresh. There was no way any of them could ever get past the freshwater barrier in the middle of the lake and reach the northern passage to escape. The Mermish Council had the Freshies trapped and imprisoned in the lake, just like they wanted.

"Okay, then." Gran pulled out a sheet of paper from the stack Ms. Wilma had given her and handed it to me as we headed out of the office. At the top it read: *New admission: Serena Finora.* "Give this to your homeroom teacher and let her know Serena is a new student. She'll have all her classes with you. Here's her class schedule, some school policy information, and this one…"

"Wait, wait. Back up the truck for a sec," I said, balancing the papers Gran had handed me. "New student? What's going on?"

"Come." Gran guided Serena and me out of the office to where Cori, Trey, and Luke were waiting. Gran shuttled us to the bench just outside the school office door.

"The thing is," Gran whispered, looking around to make sure no one was eavesdropping, "Serena's father and your parents and I have come to a bit of an agreement."

"You met Finalin?" I asked.

"Yes, such a charming fellow." Gran smoothed her slacks and looked from Serena to me. "Serena had left your necklace on that hook in the boathouse like you'd shown her, so I got your dad to come out to the cottage over the weekend to get the Merlin 3000 ready."

I'd given Serena my toe ring strung on a necklace and told her to hang it from a nail on the dock inside Gran's boathouse if she ever wanted to become human again.

"Your mom," Gran continued, "I mean, Tanti Natasha, acted as interpreter."

"Where the heck was I when all this was going on?" But

then I remembered. I'd been at Cori's, enjoying our final long weekend of summer with Luke and Trey.

"It all happened rather fast," Gran said in a low tone. "Basically, Serena's dad insists that she give being human a try again, though she wasn't thrilled by the prospect. Once I explained that she could go to school with you and your friends and be around people her own age, she seemed to warm up to the idea."

"So that's it?" I asked. "Serena is a human now?"

"Well, we've got the school part figured out for now," Gran stroked Serena's hair and smiled sweetly at her as if to reassure her that everything was as they'd agreed upon, "with the understanding that she can go home on weekends."

"Is the Merlin 3000 able to handle that?" I whispered, remembering all the trouble Dad and Eddie had setting up the mer-to-human synthesizer, which made the transition from water-breathing mer to air-breathing human easier. We hadn't even been sure it would work on Luke the first time they had used it just a few weeks before.

"Your father is making a few extra adjustments and upgrades," Gran said.

"But how are we supposed to do this, exactly?" I asked. "She can barely speak English. How is she supposed to understand anything that's going on?"

"I'm sure she'll catch on," Cori said. "She already understands a lot of English."

"But not just school," I protested, thinking about how Serena had pretty much taken over every waking moment of my life for the short time she was human the last time. "What about—"

Gran touched my arm to stop me and turned to Trey and Cori.

"Why don't you two show Serena the bulletin board?" Gran asked them with a wink. Trey gave her a thumbs-up while Cori took Serena by the arm and led her to the bulletin board and out of earshot.

"I know this is not ideal," Gran glanced around the bustling hallway, "but I'm counting on you and Luke and your friends to help make this as smooth a transition as possible. That father of hers—Finnegan, is it?"

"Finalin," I said with a shudder, remembering the merman's pockmarked face and scraggly beard.

"Well, whatever his name is, the fella has quite a temper. He's already damaged a lot of the boats in the area, and he's threatened to start wreaking more havoc around the lake if we don't cooperate."

"He's the one who cut our boat from its mooring!" Luke exclaimed. "And all that other stuff happening on the lake, I bet he's behind that, too."

So, Finalin was sabotaging boats and holding it over our heads unless we cooperated? The guy was a menace.

"Yes, and given his past performance..." Gran's voice trailed off.

I thought back to the day last summer when Finalin and his wife, Medora, had pulled Mom underwater and we all thought she'd drowned.

"Do you think he would actually hurt anyone?"

"It's quite possible," Gran said, making sure Serena wasn't listening. "All I know is that we'd better cooperate or else we might find out."

"Don't worry, Mrs. Baxter," Luke said. "We'll take care of Serena. Right, Jade?"

I glanced across the hallway. Cori took a scarf from around her neck and wrapped it around Serena's. Cori had been thrilled to have a life-sized model for her *Cori Original* designs last time Serena was human. Serena hadn't minded. In fact, she seemed to enjoy being a human Barbie doll.

"I am going to have *so* much fun dressing you again," I heard Cori exclaim.

"Well, I wouldn't want to deprive Cori of her human mannequin." I turned to Luke. "You think we can do this?"

"We can totally do this." He took my hand and squeezed it.

"Thank you, dearie." Gran patted Luke on the arm and kissed me on the cheek, then adjusted her handbag over her shoulder and headed for the school door just as the 9:00 a.m. starting bell rang. "Now be good and don't go getting yourselves into too much trouble."

"We won't," I called after her.

But given what had happened the last time me, Luke, Cori, Trey, and Serena had all been together, that "not getting into too much trouble" part seemed highly unlikely.

Chapter Three

GETTING TO HOMEROOM TOOK *forever* because
Serena held me hostage at the bulletin board outside
the school office well after everyone had scattered for their
classes. She kept pulling notices off the board and handing
them to me, wanting to know what they meant.

"That's to sign up for senior band and the other one is
about cyber-bullying, but Serena—you can't keep pulling
these things off!" I said in exasperation as I tried to find a
thumbtack to reattach a neon orange flyer advertising the
upcoming school elections. Serena took the paper from me
again and pointed to the picture of a ballot marked with an
X on the "Please Vote" option.

"It's for a school election or something," I said, layering
it over a flyer beside it so I could use the same thumbtack.

"Elec-shun?" Serena sounded out the word.

"Yeah, where everybody votes for people to represent
them on School Council." I made a lot of motions with my
hands to try to explain but I wasn't quite sure she understood.

"Sh-chool Counshill? Like Mermish Counshill?"

"Sorta kinda—but not really. Come on." I pulled on her arm to go. "We're already late."

Mrs. Thorne's classroom was at the other end of the glassed-in hallway that cut through the courtyard separating junior from senior high. Going there felt like being traded back down to the minor leagues in baseball. I rushed down the hallway hoping we wouldn't get in trouble for being late on our first day.

We finally got to homeroom at about 9:12, with only eight minutes left before our first class. Luckily for us, Mrs. Thorne was also having a rough start to her first day and was busy mopping up a mug of coffee that had spilled over a few papers on her desk. A bunch of eighth-grade boys were gathered by the window making rude noises, while a few of the girls kept undoing and redoing these weird, stacked half-ponytails on top of their heads, which they held back with skinny headbands.

They looked up at Serena and me like we were some kind of teenage aliens from another dimension. Hello? Probably because ninth graders weren't *supposed* to be in junior high! In fact, I only recognized four other poor saps from my grade, two guys and two girls. One of the girls looked even more miserable than I was.

"Lainey." I smiled as pleasant a smile as I could muster. "How are you?"

Lainey Chamberlain is the daughter of Martin Chamberlain of Chamberlain Construction—the same construction company I'd exposed in a shady political scheme at the end of the summer, which stopped their multimillion-dollar construction project at Port Toulouse Mall.

That Lainey Chamberlain.

Being stuck with eighth graders was probably the worst thing anyone could ever do to her, but Lainey looked even more unhappy that she'd been put in the same homeroom as me. Especially since we had never been in the same homeroom since her family moved to Port Toulouse back in fifth grade. What were the chances?

"Jade Baxter," Lainey sneered and glanced over at Serena. "And your cousin, right? Salina or something?"

"Laineesh!" Serena remembered Lainey from when they met at the boat canal a few weeks before. Serena had fallen in love with Lainey's teacup-sized dog, Cedric, and kind of dognapped him. "Chedrich?"

Before I could stop her, Serena was leaning over Lainey and digging into her oversized handbag, looking for Cedric.

"What the heck?" Lainey shrieked. "Get off me, you freak!"

"I'm sorry!" I stifled a laugh and pulled Serena away. "Serena, dogs aren't allowed in school." I tried to whisper so no one could hear me, forgetting that I could have just ringed to her in my mer voice. But it was too late. Lainey had heard me.

"Are dogs allowed in the school where *she* comes from?" Lainey zipped up her handbag and scowled.

By then, a dozen set of eyes were turned in our direction. One of the eighth-grade girls blew a curl from her forehead, and a guy by the window stopped mid-armpit fart. I gulped.

"Actually…" I looked around at all the expectant faces. Despite Lainey's wisecrack, I could tell most of the people staring at us hadn't made their minds up about Serena just yet. It was up to me to make sure I got her school cred on the right track.

I took a page out of Gran's book and got my imagination going.

"Every student at Tonganesia High brings a dog to school," I continued. "Dogs are very sensitive to seismic shifts in the earth's crust. Since Serena's village was at the base of an active volcano, the dogs act as alarms during the students' mile-long walk to school. Not to mention, protecting everyone from Komodo dragon attacks through the dangerous rain forest."

I had no idea if any of that actually made any sense, but a few of the eighth-grade girls gasped.

"In fact…" I paused for effect, trying to catch a few people's eyes. "Serena's dog rescued her when her town was buried by a volcanic eruption this summer. It's a miracle she's still alive."

"Whoa." One boy whacked his friend across the chest and raised an eyebrow.

Lainey Chamberlain gripped her oversized handbag closer and scanned the class, scowling when she saw everyone looking my way.

"Well, whatever," Lainey muttered. She shrugged her bag over her shoulder and took a seat at one of the desks at the back of the class. "Just keep that freak away from me."

Serena slipped into a seat next to some of the eighth-grade

girls. I dragged another desk over from a nearby row to keep an eye on her. Serena put a hand to her hair and motioned to the girls' ponytails.

"Pretteesh," she exclaimed.

A girl with a fuchsia headband smiled and pulled a few hair elastics from her pencil case. She asked Serena if she wanted her hair done, too.

"Yesh!" Serena exclaimed.

I smiled. I didn't really need to worry about Serena after all. The boys all stared at her like she was some kind of Greek goddess, and the girls were spellbound by her long, never-ever-been-cut, golden brown hair. She had the whole class (except for Lainey, of course) wrapped around her little finger just by being…Serena.

With Serena occupied, I grabbed my chance and walked up to Mrs. Thorne's desk to give her Serena's homeroom registration form like Gran had asked me.

"Great to see you back, Jade," Mrs. Thorne said in her usual cheery tone. "Your father called me to see if you could be in my homeroom again this year."

So *he* was the one to blame. Dad had obviously never been a fourteen-year-old girl desperate to start high school.

"He worried about your performance at the end of last year," Mrs. Thorne continued. "I assured him we'd keep on top of things to make sure you don't fall behind again. Sound like a plan?"

"Sure." Though it didn't sound like I had much of a choice in the matter.

"Excellent." She threw the last of the coffee-stained paper towels into the garbage can, then held out her hand for the paper I'd offered her. "I see you have a friend with you." She glanced at the name at the top of the paper. "Serena...Finora, is it?"

"Yeah, Serena's my, um, cousin." It was weird to have to keep remembering that. "She's new."

"That's great." Mrs. Thorne looked up from the paper and waved to Serena as I returned to my desk. "Welcome!"

Serena smiled and raised her hand awkwardly in a wave.

"Okay, everyone. Take your seats so I can get attendance," Mrs. Thorne addressed the rest of the class. "And welcome back for another fun-filled year."

Everyone groaned as she ticked off names on her attendance list.

"Now for a couple of morning announcements," Mrs. Thorne continued. "Eighth graders will meet at recess in the band room to discuss fundraising ideas for this year's field trip. Ninth graders, be sure to sign up for one of the many extramural sports teams added to this year's roster."

I zoned out at the mention of physical activity. One thing I'd been looking forward to with high school? No more scheduled Physical Education. Mrs. Thorne must have seen my eyes glaze over because she seemed to speak directly to me next.

"As part of Port Toulouse Regional High's new Healthy Schools Initiative, every high-schooler is required to perform four hours of scheduled physical activity per week.

The school has added several new teams to accommodate everyone's interests."

Team? Me? She couldn't be serious. Other than the punishment of elementary and junior high's twice-weekly gym class, I'd done my best to avoid any kind of organized sports since dodge ball had etched its painful memory on me in third grade. Now they were forcing me to sweat? To possibly run?

What is she saying? Serena rang to me in her mer voice.

We need to join a sports team, I rang back, sagging in my desk chair.

Sports? Serena rang.

Several students around us checked their phones or looked up at the fluorescent lights, trying to figure out the source of the buzzing noise.

I lowered my mer voice to a faint ring. *Yeah, like soccer or basketball or swimming—*

Swimming? Serena's eyes lit up.

I shouldn't have said that. "Forget I said that," I muttered.

"Also," Mrs. Thorne held up the same neon orange flyer Serena had pulled off the bulletin board earlier, "we'll be looking for a ninth-grade representative for School Council. Let me know if you're interested, and I'll register your name for next week's elections."

Since we only had thirty-five or so students per grade, we only had one grade representative instead of one for each individual class.

"Mrs. Thorne?" Lainey Chamberlain asked sweetly from

her desk at the back of the class. "It has been my pleasure representing my fellow students for the past three consecutive years, so I would be happy to continue the tradition into high school and put my name forward again this year." She tucked a strand of her perfectly straightened hair behind her ear.

"Thank you, Lainey. Your dedication is…admirable." Mrs. Thorne wrote Lainey's name in her notes. She looked up and scanned the rest of the classroom. "Anyone else?"

Serena's hand shot up as her new friend was putting the finishing touches on her ponytail.

"Oh!" I pulled Serena's hand down with an embarrassed smile. "Serena's still really new. She doesn't quite get the whole 'election' thing."

"Skull Counshell?" Serena asked.

"P-shh, as if…" Lainey smacked her lips together and snapped the top of her lip gloss closed. "She can't even say it right."

I had a sudden urge to snatch the lip gloss from Lainey's grip and crack it in two. Instead, I turned to Mrs. Thorne and managed my sweetest voice.

"But I'd be more than happy to show Serena the ropes. It would be a great way to introduce her to our way of life, improve her English, and possibly get some new talent on this year's School Council."

"Marvelous idea, Jade. I'll put her name down," Mrs. Thorne said just as the bell rang.

"Counshell?" Serena grasped my arm as we gathered up our bags to head to our first class.

"Yes, Serena. You can run for School Council."

She jumped and gave me a big hug. I had to hand it to the girl; Serena was definitely taking to this high-school thing well, though I doubted a brand-new student who could barely speak English had much of a chance against Lainey Chamberlain's three-year class president monopoly.

"Let's get one thing straight, Baxter," Lainey whispered as she brushed by me and headed out the door. "Chamberlains always come out on top. Remember that."

Okay, so maybe Serena didn't have a chance at winning, but as I watched Lainey Chamberlain flounce out into the corridor like a blond Kardashian, I figured the hissy fits alone would be worth the effort.

Chapter Four

B Y THE END OF the school day, Serena wasn't just
running for class president; she'd joined the Chess
Club, the Junior Environmentalists Club, and the female
underwater hockey team. Her newfound enthusiasm for
high school was becoming exhausting.

Thankfully, Cori volunteered to chaperone Serena at the
Junior Environmentalists Club during Monday lunch—
and Luke was going to pick up the slack with Wednesday
Chess Club— but I was stuck joining underwater hockey
with her on Tuesdays and Thursdays after school, despite
the fact that I hated swimming and had an unhealthy aver-
sion to bathing suits. (I know! A mermaid who hates the
water, but what can I say?)

I tried to convince Serena that joining a "swimming"
sport wasn't such a good idea for a teenage girl with a
mermaid secret, but she caught a glimpse of the glistening
water of the rec center's indoor pool on the way to the
cafeteria at lunchtime, and there was no talking her out
of it.

Okay, okay, I said to her in Mermish rings as we waited for the pool director, Coach Laurena, to return from answering the phone in her office. *But it doesn't matter if it's salt, fresh, or chlorine, you can never, ever, ever inhale any of the water in the pool, or you could turn back into a mermaid.*

It was okay for us mers to swim, but we had to be careful. Breathing water for more than a few seconds tripped our "mermaid switch" and then it was tail city. Breathing air did the reverse for me, forcing the change back from mermaid to human, but that change was a little more complicated for full-fledged mers like Serena, Luke, and Mom.

Serena looked up from a *Safe 2 Swim* pamphlet and stared at me blankly.

And turning back into a mermaid half a mile from an open body of water would be bad, I emphasized.

"Ba-ahhd," Serena repeated in English just as Coach Laurena came back to her desk with the sign-up sheet.

"Oh, don't worry if you don't play very well," Coach Laurena said, apparently misunderstanding the gist of our conversation. Her arm bangles jingled as she tucked her chestnut hair behind her ear. She had cut her bangs since the last time I'd seen her at Bridget's Diner, where I had worked during the summer. Her fiancé, Daniel, was the diner's head cook. "The underwater hockey team is only a year old so most of our girls are at a beginner level. I think our main focus will be developing our swimming endurance. That tended to be our weakness last year."

"Good plan," I agreed with a laugh, thinking that with Serena's participation, the Port Toulouse Regional High underwater hockey team's overall swimming level was about to improve significantly. On the other hand, I would probably even things out. But with the school's new Healthy Schools Initiative, my choice was either underwater hockey or something that involved running.

Shudder.

So, after a day of sign-ups, mix-ups, and slip-ups, the final bell couldn't come soon enough. Plus, our Social Studies teacher had already assigned a huge project due by next Friday, and Serena and I had been made partners so I'd obviously have to do most of the work. And yes— my final grades had taken kind of a nosedive at the end of eighth grade, thanks to all the mer drama unraveling smack dab in the middle of final exams. Mrs. Thorne, Dad, and Mom were watching my every move to make sure I didn't screw up again this year.

No pressure.

By the time Cori, Trey, Luke, Serena, and I had made the mile-long trek to Bridget's Diner after school, I collapsed into a corner booth, exhausted from my first day of mer-sitting. And, since Serena had held me captive in the pool office through lunch, I hadn't had a chance to eat all day.

The delicious smells of waffle fries and burgers wafting from the kitchen kicked my appetite into high gear.

"Bridget Burger with the works and as many waffle

fries as you can legally fit onto my plate, please," I said to Bridget when she came by our booth to take our orders.

"You got it." Bridget winked and filled our water glasses as everyone else placed their orders. Her face broke into a huge smile once she noticed Serena. "Hey, you're back!"

Serena smiled, too. "Hi, Bridg-shet."

"Yeah," I piped up. "Serena and her mom are living with us for now. She gets to see her dad on the weekends, though." That would sound pretty normal if Serena were just another one of my friends from school. A few kids I knew had parents who were separated, and they went to a dad's or mom's on the weekend, but I doubted any of them spent their weekends at the bottom of Talisman Lake.

"Well, it's wonderful to have you back." Bridget nodded in understanding. "And perfect timing, too. Our cook, Daniel, has a clam recipe he's been dying to try."

Bridget had no idea about our secret mer identities, but I'd managed to convince her that Serena's picky eating habits were because she was from a remote island in the South Pacific. Daniel had made Serena steamed mussels last time and they'd been a big hit.

Clam? Serena rang and looked at me, confused.

I leaned over and rang quietly in her ear. *They're like the mussels you had last time.*

"Kind of like the mussels you had last time," Bridget said as she continued writing our orders on her notepad. "You're gonna love them."

I looked up, shocked. How could Bridget know what

I'd ringed to Serena in my mer voice? Had I actually said it out loud? I glanced at Luke but he gave me a quick shake of the head as if to say not to worry. I looked back at Bridget but she gave no indication that she'd heard me either.

"Thank shoe," Serena said to Bridget.

"You are very welcome. In fact, it's so nice to see you *all* back," Bridget said as she walked back to the counter to attach our orders to the revolving carousel at the order window. She was limping slightly and looked tired. "Things have been quiet since we closed up the ice cream parlor after tourist season."

"Yeah," I said. Cori and I had worked at the ice cream parlor all summer. "I miss coming in here every day, too. The ice cream perks were kinda sweet."

"You were two of my best scoopers," Bridget called from the counter. "No offense to Chelse, of course."

I smiled, remembering how clueless Chelse Becker had been about running an ice cream parlor but she more than made up for it with her texting superiority.

"Chelse?" Serena asked. She and Chelse had been secret friends since they were kids, getting together when Chelse vacationed at her family's summer cottage in Dundee.

"She's only here in the summertime," Cori piped up, "but I have her cell number. We can text her if you want."

Serena had no clue what "texting" was, but we swapped seats so Cori could show her.

Bridget spun the order carousel and rang the bell for Daniel. "Okay. Your orders should be ready in a few minutes."

"Good, because I am starving," I said.

"Me, too," Luke agreed. "That cafeteria food is nothing to write home about."

"As least you got lunch," I complained.

We sat around for the next ten minutes or so, comparing school schedules and talking about the upcoming school events.

"So, Serena is all signed up to run for ninth-grade rep," I said casually.

"Counshell," Serena said, looking up from Cori's phone.

"That's so cool," Cori said. "Good for you, Serena."

"Against Lainey Chamberlain," I continued.

"Oh, ouch," Trey said. "How did that go over?"

"Yeah," Luke added. "Is Lainey still angry about the fact we basically ruined her father's company with that whole mall-construction thing?"

"Oh, I don't think Chamberlain Construction is ruined," Trey said. "The mall extension is still being built, just away from the tidal pool like we fought for. And Chamberlain Construction got the contract."

"Are you kidding me?" I asked. We'd basically exposed Chamberlain Construction's history of bribes and shoddy business practices, and they *still* kept their construction contract? I guess what Lainey said was true: Chamberlains always *did* come out on top.

"In fact, last time I was at the mall, Chamberlain Construction had a big display at Sport Mart, giving out free bathing caps," Trey continued. "Some kind of *Safe 2 Swim* promotion or something."

"That's that swim program they've had at the pool for the past few years," Cori said.

"So now what? Chamberlain Construction is giving away freebies all of a sudden?" I muttered. "They're just trying to get in everyone's good books after scamming us with that fake environmental assessment."

"I dunno, Jade," Luke said. "Maybe it's for real. They just installed new lifeguard towers at the beach last week. I'm pretty sure Chamberlain Construction sponsored those, too."

"Yeah, so they could put their signs all over them, probably," I muttered.

Just then, Luke and Trey's grandfather, Shaky Eddie, entered the diner. Eddie used to be a professor at a university in Florida until he was laughed off the faculty for publishing a scientific paper about a mer discovery. He was still the best mer expert I knew, but now he preferred to keep his knowledge a secret and encouraged us all to do the same.

"Hey, Grandpa," Luke called over. "Taking a break?"

Eddie was the canal's lock master. He controlled the metal gates that let boats travel back and forth from Talisman Lake to the Atlantic Ocean. Eddie smiled and strolled over to our table.

"Yeah, things have been a little slow. Haven't had a boat go through all week. You young people start school already?" Eddie pointed at our backpacks but seemed distracted as he glanced at the front door, then to Bridget, who'd returned to the counter. She waved and poured him a cup of coffee.

"Yeah, back to the grind," Trey said.

"They're waiting for you in the back office," Bridget whispered as she walked by. She nodded to the hallway leading to the office and handed Eddie the cup of coffee. "I'll be there in a sec."

"That was weird," Trey said as he watched his grandfather retreat to the back office with his mug while Bridget cleared off the table by the door and brought the dirty dishes back to the kitchen.

"Yeah," Luke agreed. "I wonder what's going on back there."

After a few more minutes, my stomach grumbled and I looked at my watch, wondering why our food was taking so long.

"I'm going to go check on our orders before I gnaw off my arm," I said as I slid out of the booth.

"Good plan," Cori agreed, joining me.

The orders were all lined up at the order window when we got there, but there was no sign of Bridget. We'd worked at the diner's ice cream parlor long enough to know that Bridget prided herself on getting the food to the table piping hot.

"Do you think she would mind?" Cori asked, reading my mind.

I picked up a few of the plates and headed back to our booth.

"Wouldn't hurt to move things along," I replied, imagining biting into a thick, juicy burger. "It's like we're doing her a favor."

Cori followed me back to the booth with the other plates, but by the time we'd placed them on the table, it was obvious we were missing my Bridget Burger and extra waffle fries.

Luke shook salt all over his french fries, then took the top off his bun and shook even more salt onto it.

"Not salty enough for you?" I asked.

"I don't know what it is, but food just doesn't have any taste these days." He placed the shaker back on the table and looked over to my spot. "Where's your order?"

"They were one short. It'll probably be up in a minute." I glanced toward the order window, but there was still no one in sight.

"Here, take mine," Luke offered and pushed his plate toward me. Give up his food for me? He really was the perfect guy. But secretly, I really wanted those extra waffle fries, and a quarter of Luke's plate was taken up by a perfectly useless dish of coleslaw.

Plus, all that salt! What was up with that?

"Naw, thanks anyway." I stole a fry from the outer edge of his plate, hoping it had escaped most of the salt shaker's wrath. "I'll just go check and see what's happening with mine."

I popped my head through the order window into the kitchen, but Daniel and Bridget were nowhere to be found, so I headed to the back office.

"Hey, Bridget?" I asked, knocking lightly and pushing the office door open a smidge so she'd hear me.

"Is that Jade?" I heard my mother say.

I opened the door a little more. There in Bridget's office were Bridget, Mom, Dad, Eddie, Daniel (who really should have been making my waffle fries just then), and his fiancée, Coach Laurena.

"Um, hi!" I worked to try to make sense of the group. What were they all doing, meeting together like this? "What's up?"

"Jade, come in," Mom said.

"I'm not sure that's a good idea," Dad whispered but loud enough for me to hear. Honestly, it was a miracle he didn't spell out the words like when I was four; it was that obvious they were hiding something.

I glanced from face to face as they sat on folding chairs scattered around Bridget's office.

"Don't be silly, Dal. She's one of us." Mom stood and took me by the shoulders and addressed the rest of the group. "For those who don't know, this is Jade."

Coach Laurena smiled and waved in acknowledgment since we'd met at the pool office just a few hours before. Daniel waved as well.

"Okay…" I considered their faces for a second. Did this have something to do with school? The diner? Mom, Dad, and Eddie knew about the mermaid stuff, but surely that wasn't what this meeting was all about.

"Are you guys…" But I didn't want to finish the

sentence unless I knew for sure. One of the big rules about being a mer was that you kept the secret to yourself. Our Mer Code of Silence was the only way mers had been able to survive without being discovered.

Bridget stood up first. "I guess this is as good a time as any. We're going to need as much help as we can get, given the circumstances."

"Circumstances?" I looked from Bridget to Mom and Dad, trying to get a hint of what was going on. "Okay, somebody needs to clue me in on what's really happening here."

Eddie cleared his throat.

"Well, maybe this will help." He turned to the group. "Will all the mers in the room please raise their hands?"

Mom was the first to do so, then Coach Laurena and finally Bridget.

"Coach Laurena?" I asked with a gasp. My underwater hockey coach was a mermaid? "Bridget?" I said even louder.

All the time I'd been working at the diner's ice cream parlor that summer I'd been trying to hide my secret from Bridget. And now I found out she was a mermaid, too? But the more I thought about it, the more it all made sense.

"You're a mer, too?" I looked over at Bridget and blinked a few times. "That's how you knew how important the tidal pool behind the mall was."

"Yep. It had taken me a while to find it again after I transformed, but once I did, it became pretty important to me, too," Bridget said with a smile. "Been a Webbed One for about fifteen years now." "Webbed One" was the term for a human who started off as a mer.

"And Coach Laurena?" I turned to her.

"Three years this summer." Coach Laurena placed a hand on Daniel's shoulder and turned to me with a mischievous smile.

Back in June, I'd thought I was the only land-dwelling mer on the planet. Now I was staring, mouth open, at Mom plus Bridget and Laurena. Not to mention my mer-guy, Luke, eating his extremely salty fries back in the diner. Four other mers.

My mind was officially blown.

"Wow." My knees wobbled. "I need to sit down."

I reached out to steady myself to keep from passing out and knocked over a pile of new stainless-steel pots, scattering them all over the floor.

Chapter Five

T HE SOUND OF CRASHING pots brought Cori, Trey, Luke, and Serena to the office, wondering what the heck was going on.

Eddie tried to explain what was happening while Bridget made sure there were no new customers in the diner so she could lock the front door.

"Wait just a sec. Let me get this straight." Cori held up a hand and closed her eyes as if trying to solve a quadratic equation in her head. We had all squeezed into the diner office and were standing, sitting, or perched on any available surface. "Who exactly are the humans and who are the mers here?"

I pretended I was a talk-show host and grabbed a spatula to serve as my microphone.

"Well, on Team Tail we have: Jade, Serena, Luke, my mom, Coach Laurena—" I pointed to each of them as I spoke.

Just then, Bridget returned to the office. "And don't forget about me."

"Bridget?" Cori put a hand to her mouth in disbelief. Bridget laughed and put an arm around Cori's shoulder.

"And on the leg team—" I began.

"You've got Dalrymple Baxter, the husband and doting dad," Dad piped up.

"Chef Daniel, the dashing fiancé," chimed in Daniel, flashing a smile.

"And I'm the old guy who drinks too much coffee." Shaky Eddie lifted his trembling mug.

"So," Bridget stood at her desk as if addressing a classroom, "we've all gathered here today because we've got ourselves a problem on the mer front."

"You mean all the vandalism happening on Talisman Lake?" I remembered what Gran and Luke had said about the sunken Jet Skis and damaged boats. "I thought we'd figured out *Whatcha-ma-call-him* was behind that."

I tried to be vague so Serena wouldn't catch on to the fact that her dad was to blame for the shenanigans around the lake. Serena may have been the daughter of one of the vilest mers on the planet, but he was still her dad.

"No," Bridget said. "This isn't about Talisman Lake, though we're sure hoping that problem is under control."

Serena looked from me to Bridget, trying to keep up with the conversation. Mom put a hand on Serena's shoulder and whispered something in her ear.

"This new situation is more ocean-side," Bridget continued while Mom translated everything for Serena in mer rings. "The truth is, the Mermish Council has decided to recall all land-dwelling mers."

A murmur rose from the group as everyone looked at each other, wondering what this meant.

"Recall?" I asked.

"They're ordering all the Webbed Ones back to the ocean," Bridget said quietly.

Webbed Ones were humans who started off as mers, like Mom, Bridget, Laurena, Serena, and Luke. I started off as a human with mermaid tendencies so my situation was not quite the same as everyone else's, but still—this was not good news.

Most mer people thought Webbed Ones were just part of the fairy tales they were told when they were kids. The Mermish Council worked very hard to keep it that way to prevent ocean mers from defecting to land all willy-nilly.

"But…" A large knot formed at the back of my throat as I tried to make sense of what was happening. "Why would the Mermish Council do that?"

"There's been some fighting between the Mermish Council and a group of mers who aren't happy with the Council's policies," Eddie said.

Mom continued to ring the mer translation to Serena. Her eyes grew wide.

It's like what Uncle Alzear told us before they locked us in the lake, Serena rang excitedly to me. *Alzear talked about an uprising, remember? He said some mers would stop at nothing to see the Freshies free again.*

All the mers in the room looked over to Serena, while the non-mers searched our faces to try to understand what Serena had just said.

"Serena's right," Luke chimed in. "Uncle Alzear told us a group of mers were starting some kind of secret revolution."

Uncle Alzear was Luke and our mer-friend Reese's uncle and a sentry guard for the Mermish Council.

"Well, the same underground—or *underwater*—revolution is gaining momentum," Bridget said. "But the Mermish Council members are imprisoning everyone who opposes them in Talisman Lake with the rest of the Freshies."

"That's nothing new," I said, remembering the underwater tribunal when the Mermish Council had captured Luke. "Dame Council practically admitted that Serena's parents were framed for a murder they didn't commit because they had spoken out against the Council. Apparently, a lot of the Freshies in Talisman Lake are there for the same reason."

Serena gave me a grateful smile.

Eddie chimed in. "About seven mers are being held at the canal by the sentries right now. They're waiting for me to open the gate's lock when the next boat comes through. That's more prisoners than I've seen in the past three years."

"So where does this recall thing come in?" I asked. "If the Mermish Council is kicking its enemies out of the ocean, doesn't that kind of solve the Council's problem?"

"Seven mers is just the tip of the iceberg," Bridget said quietly. "Many more mers are secretly unhappy, and the

Council members want to make sure they're ready for any more surprises. According to my source, the Mermish Council is revoking land status and drafting Webbed Ones into their forces to help fight the uprisings."

"What?" I cried. "That's crazy. They can't do that."

If all the Webbed Ones I knew were recalled to the ocean to fight for the Mermish Council that would mean losing Luke, Serena, Bridget, and...Mom. Plus Coach Laurena and any other Webbed Ones walking around Port Toulouse that we didn't already know about.

"Yeah, it's not like they can force us to jump back into the ocean if we don't want to," Luke said.

"Right," I agreed. "What are they going to do—come pull us from our beds?"

"Well, not exactly," Bridget said. "But mers are governed by very powerful ancient laws. For instance, haven't you ever had an urge to rescue a human in need?"

A light turned on inside my brain. "Yes! Like that time Cori fell into the ocean down at Toulouse Point. And the other time she fell off the truck at the construction site."

"I really need to stop falling off stuff," Cori joked.

"Is that the kind of thing you mean?" I asked Bridget.

"Yes," Bridget said. "These are forces we have no control over. This time, the Mermish Council plans to enforce Tidal Law, which is basically like recalling all the aliens to the mother ship."

"Huh?" I asked.

"It's like we all have GPS trackers inside us, and when

the Mermish Council members want to call us back, they switch on their homing device to lead us there," Mom answered. "Every mer reacts to Tidal Law in a different way, but there's no way we can fight against it if that's what the Mermish Council wants."

"But Tidal Law? What do tides have to do with anything?" I asked.

"Nature is a powerful thing," Dad chimed in, putting on his engineering hat. "If we've learned anything from our research on tidal pools, it's that we can't make any assumptions."

Dad had a point. The tides in the tidal pool behind the mall had helped Mom and Serena become human by controlling the right amount of air and water and salt they breathed to force the change. Dad had invented the Merlin 3000 in our garage as a prototype that did the same thing, using a hot tub, computers, and a bunch of tubes.

"So, when is this supposed to happen?" I asked.

"If my source is correct, they plan on using the next supermoon when the tides are the strongest to help them." Bridget glanced at the calendar.

"What's a supermoon?" I asked.

"There's a full moon every month or so, but every fourteen months the moon's orbit brings it closest to the earth, making the full moon seem larger than normal," Dad chimed in. "It also creates really high tides."

"They've been waiting for this opportunity for a while now," Bridget said. "The supermoon and the high tides will create the best conditions for whatever they have planned."

"But even if they get us in the ocean, they can't force us to fight for them," Luke insisted.

"Apparently they have some secret weapon they plan to use to control us but again, they're waiting for the supermoon to take full effect so they can get the best bang for their buck," Bridget added.

"And they're locking up anyone causing them grief in the meantime," Eddie added.

"But we have time to figure out how to beat this, right?" I asked. "When's the next supermoon?"

"Just hold on a sec and I'll tell you." Dad was already googling for the answer on his phone. "Oh, this is interesting. Did you know the word 'lunatic' is derived from the word 'luna,' which is Latin for moon? Some believe full moons can have profound psychological—"

"Dad!"

"Nine days." Dad clicked off his phone and put it in his belt holder. "The next supermoon is nine days away."

"Nine days!" I cried. This couldn't be happening. I'd just started dating and had finally made it to high school. Weren't those the kind of things I should be worried about instead of being forced to fight in a marine war? "Why would the Mermish Council want Webbed Ones in the ocean again, anyway? So far, the Council has done everything it can to keep them a secret."

"They're obviously getting desperate," Dad said.

Dad put his arm around Mom's shoulder and laid his cheek against her hair. Just when I'd gotten our family back together, now the Mermish Council wanted to tear it apart again? No way!

"This is all ridiculous," I said with a shake of my head. "I still don't see how the moon can be used to control someone."

"Interesting fact…" Dad pushed his glasses back up his nose and blinked quickly. "There's actual scientific evidence that lunar phases have a physiological effect on human biological functions at the cellular level."

"Thanks, Dad," I muttered. "That really clears things up."

"Maybe I can help." Bridget pulled a few metal thumbtacks off her bulletin board and grabbed a large cooking pot I'd toppled over. "Come to the kitchen and I'll show you."

We all filed into the kitchen as Bridget put an inch of water into the pot at the big sink. She dropped a bunch of tacks into the pot and pulled the heavy-duty magnet that held the food purchase orders off the kitchen fridge. We gathered around the sink to watch.

"The moon acts like a big magnet over the water." She held the magnet a short distance away from the water. The tacks jiggled in response. "The closer the moon is to the earth, like during a supermoon, the stronger the magnetic pull." She hovered the magnet closer to the water and waved it over the thumbtacks. They followed the magnet's path.

"Even if we don't see the forces of the tide and moon, they still control us," she continued. "The Mermish Council has somehow found a way to harness this power and use it to its advantage."

Everyone talked among themselves as they discussed what this all meant. Finally, Eddie piped up.

"So basically, we have nine days to figure out how to deal with this. We just wanted you to be aware of what's going on so we can try to prepare the best we can."

"So what do we do in the meantime?" Coach Laurena asked. "I've got all the school teams to manage plus the fall aquatic program for the community center." She grasped Daniel's hand.

"School Counshell?" Serena asked. "Hockshee? Chessh Club—"

"Chess Club?" Mom and Dad looked at me and back to Serena.

"Yeah, Serena's been bitten by the school spirit bug," I said.

"I think the best thing to do is go about your business for now," Eddie said. "Dalrymple and I will do more research on the subject. But if anything happens out of the ordinary in the meantime, report it back to us."

Everyone shifted in their spots, not quite knowing what to do next.

"And I'll try to get more information from my source," Bridget said. "In the meantime, how about if Daniel and I fry up some clams for everyone to let all this information sink in?"

"I'm on it." Daniel opened the fridge door and started pulling things out. Everyone nodded in agreement and headed back out into the diner. I held back.

"Hey, Bridget?" I asked once everyone else had gone. "Who exactly is this source you keep talking about?"

"My son." Bridget put the thumbtacks aside and dumped the water from the pot.

"I never knew you had a son," I said in surprise. In all the years I'd known Bridget, she'd never once mentioned any kind of family.

"We all have our secrets, don't we?" Bridget dried her hands and looked at me for a moment, then went to her coat hanging on the hook by the back door. She pulled a familiar-looking ID folder from her coat's pocket, then walked back over to me and opened the folder's flap.

She turned the picture toward me. "I believe you kids call him Reese?"

It was an underwater close-up shot of a teenager's face. Sure enough, through the shimmering water in the picture, the chubby, cheerful face of a teenage mer-boy I knew smiled back.

Reese!

Reese had told me that he'd lost his mother but that he always carried her memory around. Suddenly it all made sense.

"So that's why Reese carries your picture in his satchel. He has one of these ID folders, too. I thought he was a klepto, but you're actually his mom?"

"Yup. I had to give him up as soon as he was born. We've stayed in touch ever since, but it's been hard."

"Ah, man." My mind was about to explode from information overload.

"Are you okay?" Bridget asked, reaching out to touch my arm.

"Yes, but if you don't mind, can I pass on the clams? What I could really use is the biggest Bridget Burger known to man."

Chapter Six

BREAKFAST WAS TENSER THAN usual the next morning after everything that had happened at Bridget's Diner the day before. We sat around the kitchen table, trying to come up with a plan to deal with the possibility that everyone might be dragged back to sea in just over a week.

Another thing throwing us off kilter was having the fourth seat at the breakfast table occupied by a new member of the Baxter family. But instead of looking worried, Serena looked positively blissful about the prospect of a looming mer revolution. She even tried some eggs instead of her canned sardine standby.

Dad was freaking, though. He stood quickly from the table with his plate of half-eaten bacon, which, for Dad's— ahem—healthy appetite, showed exactly how upset he was.

"We'll just build some sort of safe house until this thing blows over," Dad said as he scraped his leftovers into the garbage can.

"A safe house?" I asked. "Like when the FBI puts someone in the witness protection program?"

"Not exactly. I was thinking of something more high-tech." Dad's work as an engineer had come in handy when he built us the Merlin 3000. He was obviously back in "mad scientist" mode. "I might be able to use one of our wind tunnels at work to create some kind of reverse force field. Maybe line the tunnel with anti-magnetic foil to block the forces of the moon?"

I wasn't sure his brilliant intellect was going to get us out of this one, though.

"This is the moon we're talking about, Dad. Not a fridge magnet," I said.

Dad's nervous babbling and enthusiastic plate scraping had me stressed out, too. I pushed my hash browns around my plate and tried to settle the roiling feeling in my gut that came from thinking about the Mermish Council's plan.

Serena munched on her breakfast and leafed through the Social Studies books I'd taken out of the library for our school project. She still couldn't read, but she'd stared at the pictures and made me explain everything as we worked on our project together the night before. I'd never seen anyone so excited about "Rights and Responsibilities of Good Citizenship."

"Dalrymple, honey," Mom said to Dad as she circled the next supermoon on our kitchen calendar with a red Sharpie marker. Thursday, September 17. Eight days before my life came crashing (or splashing) down around me. "Mermish Laws have been governing our species for hundreds of thousands of years. I'm not sure there's a scientific solution to this problem. Plus, we can't bring your work into this. That would definitely raise suspicion, don't you think?"

Dad returned to the table and sat down heavily. He leaned back against his chair and rubbed his hand over his head like he always did when he was upset.

"Well, then we'll just get a big bus and drive everyone to the middle of the country, far away from the ocean, and wait it out," he suggested.

"And then what?" Mom said quietly, reaching for Dad's hand. "What about the next full moon? And the next? We can't run away from this."

"So, what are we going to do?" Dad looked from Mom to me, then to Serena, then grabbed the jam jar from the middle of the table to soothe his worries with a piece of toast. "Because there's no way I'm losing you guys now that I've got you all back under one roof."

Dad struggled to get the jam jar's lid open, then gave up and set it back on the table. His face crumpled, and I knew he was about to lose it.

"Don't worry, Dad." I twisted open the jar and spread jam over a piece of toast for him. "We're not going anywhere. Who would open all the jars if we were gone?"

Serena continued to take hair-styling tips from the eighth graders in our homeroom, and in a matter of days, half a dozen or so ninth graders were wearing their hair the same way. Serena could still barely speak English, but with her easy smile and enthusiastic attitude, kids flocked to her like preschoolers fighting over a newborn kitten.

Without even trying, she had drafted a dozen new friends to help with her campaign for the next week's school election, and by lunchtime on Wednesday, the hallways were filled with her colorful campaign signs.

"It looks like a fourth grader colored them," I heard Lainey Chamberlain mutter to one of her friends as she taped one of her own professionally silk-screened campaign signs to the wall as Cori and I walked with Serena to meet Luke for Chess Club. Honestly, Lainey looked like she was running for city mayor rather than ninth-grade rep, but if Trey's story about her father's resurrected mall project was any indication, Chamberlains didn't exactly believe in doing anything halfway.

"Let it go," Cori whispered, sensing me tense up. Lainey had been getting her digs in all day with her snarky remarks.

I was mentally rehearsing telling Lainey that spending a fortune getting signs silk-screened to run for class president was a desperate cry for help, but before I could line up all the words in my head, I heard the creak of Ms. Wilma's office chair.

"Oh, Jade, honey?" Ms. Wilma poked her head out of the school office door and called to me. "And Serena. Good. Can you ladies come in here for a second?"

I stopped, inwardly cringing and hoping Ms. Wilma hadn't heard about Serena's episode with the slushie machine in the cafeteria or how she'd tried to kidnap the betta fish in Mr. Pagliaro's class so she could release it in the ocean.

"Yes?" I asked, walking into the office with Serena and Cori and bracing myself for whatever Ms. Wilma had to say.

"I've been trying to get your grandmother on the phone—can you remind her to bring Serena's school records to bingo for me?" She waved a file folder in the air, which I could only imagine was Serena's mostly empty school file. "The county is cracking down on paperwork, and the Boss Lady wants all the t's crossed and the i's dotted for new registrations."

"Sure, no problem." I faked a smile. But how exactly were we supposed to turn in school records when the only school Serena had ever been a part of was a school of mers? I tried to catch Serena's eye, but she was too busy studying the map of Port Toulouse and Talisman Lake again. What was up with Serena's fascination with maps?

I pulled Serena by the arm and headed for the door. "I'll make sure to get Gran on that right away."

"As soon as you can, okay?" Ms. Wilma rolled her chair to the door with us and glanced toward Principal Reamer's office. "As you know, without those records we won't be able to register Serena for school. That would be a shame."

"Sure thing," I said as we made our getaway, but as Ms. Wilma wheeled away, I noticed Lainey Chamberlain looking over from where she was hanging her poster on the bulletin board. Lainey smirked, her brain gears turning so fast that I was sure I could see smoke.

Great. Just what we needed—the fact that Serena's registration was at risk on Lainey's mental radar.

"Hey, Lainey! Looks like your campaign is going well," I said. Yes, I was tired of Lainey's bad attitude, but I had to distract her from what she'd just heard.

Lainey's mouth twitched slightly.

"My campaign couldn't be going better." She ripped off a piece of masking tape from the roll with her teeth and plastered it onto the poster. A wry smile grew on her lips. "But, honestly the school election is the least of my worries. I've been more focused on helping the planning committee with the upcoming Fall Folly. I really can't decide what I should wear. What will you be wearing, Jade?"

Fall Folly? What was that? It sounded familiar but I couldn't quite figure out why. Was that some kind of party or dance? And why should I worry about wearing anything in particular? All the lame school dances I'd ever been to didn't require anything more than a clean pair of jeans and a stain-free T-shirt. I glanced at Cori, who gave me a weak smile as if she knew something but wasn't telling me.

"I've got an idea!" Lainey continued in her high-pitched squeal that reminded me of the talking Barbie I used to have as a kid. "Why don't you come by Mother's boutique?"

Mrs. Chamberlain was a clothing designer and had a fancy boutique in the completed part of the new wing of Port Toulouse Mall, thanks to Mr. Chamberlain's construction company's contract.

"Oh…that won't work." Lainey waved her finger at

Serena and Cori's outfits. "We could probably rescue these two fashion disasters, but I don't think Mother stocks plus sizes for you, Jade..."

And there it was. It didn't matter that I knew Lainey was only poking fun at my size because she was being a total turd and trying to get under my skin. It still pulled me down and inward to a place where I wanted to disappear. Instead, I did the next best thing.

I shot off my mouth.

"Listen up, you lip-glossed mouth breather!" I yelled, then motioned to Cori and Serena. "These outfits are *Cori Originals*. The same designs your mom said were *amazing* when she reviewed Cori's portfolio last year."

I felt my rampage gaining steam.

"Also," I continued, "if you think for one second that you have a chance against Serena in this election, you can just go ahead and slip one of those designer shoes off your feet and beat yourself senseless with the pointy end because it is *so on*!"

Serena blinked wildly, looking from me to Cori to Lainey, not really understanding what was going on. If Finalin wanted his daughter to have a "real" high-school experience, we were off to a very good start!

I stalked away before I actually yanked off Lainey's shoe and carried out my suggestion. Serena and Cori chased after me.

"Hey," Cori said, grasping my arm for me to stop. "Don't let that jerk get to you."

"I know, I know, she's just being an idiot." I stopped to take a few deep breaths to calm down and did my best to keep from crying. "But what is she talking about? What's this Fall Folly thing and why would I have to worry about what I have to wear?"

"Don't freak out," Cori said.

"Freak out about what?" This couldn't be good.

"It's just the fall formal dance," Cori said casually. "I didn't mention it because I know how you get about anything to do with clothes shopping."

It was true. I'd practically had a nervous breakdown in the middle of Hyde's Department Store trying to find a bathing suit with Cori that past June. I shuddered at the thought of standing in front of the dressing room's three-way-mirror Cone of Truth.

"Well, that's easy. If Luke asks me to go, I'll just tell him no thanks," I said matter-of-factly.

"Yeah…the other part is that it's a 'folly' dance," Cori said.

"What's a 'folly' dance?" I asked cautiously.

"It's named after the first female sailor from Port Toulouse. This Folly Porthouse lady crossed the Atlantic Ocean with her sailboat after the Second World War to get her fiancé instead of waiting for the Navy to bring him back."

"*Fortune's Folly*? The ship that sank in Folly Passage?" I asked, remembering Gran's story. "The captain was actually a woman?"

"Yeah, it's kind of a 'girl power' story, so every fall, the high school starts off the year with a dance in her honor where the girl asks the guy out," Cori said. "I'm already going with Trey and…"

"And what?" I asked.

"Luke was standing right there when I asked Trey."

"Oh," I replied. It hadn't occurred to me that now I had an official boyfriend, I'd have to go on actual dates with him. So far we'd just done a lot of hanging out as a group. Me and Luke, Cori and Trey, going to the movies, hanging out at Mug Glug's, going to the skate park…it had been so easy. And so normal—nothing quite as drastic as a formal dance with frou-frou dresses and awkward dancing in uncomfortable shoes.

What would happen if I just didn't ask Luke to the dance? Would his feelings get hurt? Would he care?

"So you mean I need to dress up in some fancy dress and ask a guy out to what can only be described as the least appealing night of my life, all in the name of *girl power*?" I asked.

"Something like that," Cori said.

"Right." I considered everything *wrong* with that picture. "Why do I get the feeling this has all the makings of a good shipwreck?"

Chapter Seven

I PLAYED OVER MY CONVERSATION with Lainey Chamberlain about a million times in my head. Something kept nagging at me, other than her "plus size" jab. I finally clued in to what it was when Gran and Mom took Serena and me to the mall later that day so we could get stuff for our first underwater hockey practice.

"Are you sure you don't want to come in with us?" Mom asked as we stopped in front of Sport Mart and perused the list Coach Laurena had given us. We'd been venturing out more and more with Mom now that people thought she was my aunt and Serena's mom. Everyone bought the cover so far, especially with Mom's long dark hair now cropped in a bleach-blond pixie cut and with the funky glasses she'd started wearing lately.

"A Speedo is a Speedo. Can you just pick up my size?" I was a little peeved that I had to go bathing-suit shopping in the first place, but I couldn't find my tankini anywhere, despite searching high and low through my closet and drawers. "There's actually something I really need to do."

"If you're sure," Mom said as Gran showed Serena how to push through the turnstile entry into the sporting-goods store. "But come find us once you're done, okay?"

"Will do," I replied, then spotted the Chamberlain Construction *Safe 2 Swim* display with the free bathing caps. "Oh, and grab a bunch of those for our team in the meantime, could you? As long as Mr. Chamberlain hasn't started charging for them to fund his new wing."

I turned toward the newly built mall extension past Hyde's Department Store.

As much as I had tried to block it from my mind, walking through the mall reminded me of when Cori and I had shopped for that tankini at Hyde's in June. Cori was having her first-ever pool party, and she'd really wanted me to get a bathing suit so I could come. Turns out it was a surprise party in my honor to take my mind off the anniversary of Mom's "drowning" and to celebrate my fourteenth birthday.

That's how awesome Cori was.

Cori wasn't just an awesome friend—she was also really talented. So talented that Lainey's mom, Mrs. Chamberlain, had reviewed her *Cori Original* portfolio and said she loved her designs. She was even considering Cori for a mentorship.

But Cori hadn't heard from Mrs. Chamberlain since, and hearing Lainey diss Cori's designs earlier made me wonder whether it was mostly my fault that things had turned out the way they had.

It was time to set things right.

Large panels of advertising announced the new stores being introduced to the mall, but several were open already. A lot of work still needed to be done, but the Rainforest Cafe was already buzzing with a growing dinner crowd, and a gift shop and a nutrition store were fully stocked and operational.

Wow. Chamberlain Construction had obviously recovered from having to change their construction plan. I walked past the framework for a fountain where workers were scraping mortar on ceramic tiles while skids full of drywall were being wheeled into an empty storefront.

Finally, I stood in front of a window display of teeny-waisted mannequins dressed in draping fabrics with gauzy tulle puddled at their feet.

Boutique Chambre Laine

The last store I ever thought I'd enter.

I spotted Mrs. Chamberlain at the back of the store near a sewer's mannequin. She wore a beautiful gray tailored skirt and a ruffled cream-colored blouse and had her hair pulled back in a low chignon. She pinned a piece of fabric onto the beginnings of a jacket to form a sleeve while one of her associates brought an outfit to someone in the dressing room. Several other customers browsed the *New for Fall* rack.

"*Bonjour*," Mrs. Chamberlain said when she saw me.

She took a pin from her mouth and tucked it onto the lapel of her blouse. "May I be of *assistance*?"

The French accent threw me off. I blinked three times and turned to look at a rack of scarves. I realized I must seem rude for not replying, but my mind had dumped all its thoughts, and I had no real clue why I'd entered the store. How had I not known Mrs. Chamberlain was French? Then again, had I ever spoken to her? What else didn't I know about Lainey and her family?

"Uh, um…" I began, trying to recover. "I never shop in places like this."

Great. *Much* more polite.

"Oh, *ma chère*. Why not?" Mrs. Chamberlain asked kindly. "Every girl could use some sparkle in her life, *non*?"

"I guess I'm not really a sparkle kind of girl," I muttered.

"There is a special occasion, perhaps?" Mrs. Chamberlain prodded.

I thought about the Fall Folly.

"Well, there *is* a dance at school but you probably don't have anything in my size."

"Oh, surely I have *quelque chose* for you! Your skin tone is beautiful." Mrs. Chamberlain stood squarely in front of me and eyed me closely. "I see you in a jewel tone. Possibly blue, *oui*?"

Think, Jade, think. I was not there to talk about dresses; I was there to talk about Cori. I hadn't even invited Luke to the Fall Folly anyway, and the thought of it made me want to puke.

"*Non!*" I replied. Geesh. Mrs. Chamberlain probably thought I had been raised by wolves, but she'd obviously misunderstood the reason for my visit, and I had to get the conversation back on track.

But first I had to clear the air.

"I mean…I don't know if you recognize me, but I'm Jade Baxter. I caused a lot of problems for your family this summer when I told everyone about the fake environmental assessment for this mall extension."

"Ah, *Mademoiselle Baxteur?*" A look of recognition crossed Mrs. Chamberlain's face.

"Yes, but trust me, I was trying to protect that tidal pool for a very important reason. Although I know that's one of the big reasons why your daughter, Lainey, and I don't get along."

"You are not friends with my daughter?" Mrs. Chamberlain said. "But—Jade *Baxteur*—she speaks of you. How you are so funny."

Lainey Chamberlain talked to her mom about me? That was a surprise.

"Well," I said, almost losing my train of thought. "Sorry. That's not exactly why I'm here. I just came here on behalf of my friend. Cori Blake?"

"*Mademoiselle* Blake is in need of a dress?" Mrs. Chamberlain looked confused.

"No, no. You looked at Cori's fashion portfolio back in the spring."

"Ah, *oui!* Cori!" Mrs. Chamberlain replied. "She is talented. Very talented indeed!"

"And since Cori helped with the protest against your husband's company, I really hope that won't affect your decision to mentor her for our school's work-study program. She really admires you—"

"But, it has not affected a thing! I had hoped Cori would come to me for *mentoré*, what is the name? But I have not heard from her."

A spark of hope rose in my chest. Was Mrs. Chamberlain still considering Cori for the mentorship? But why hadn't she heard anything?

"You mean, she still has a chance?" I asked.

"Why, yes! I asked Lainey to give her the, *mon Dieu*, how you say—paperwork?" Mrs. Chamberlain said. "Lainey was to tell Cori to telephone me, but she says she has not yet spoken to her?"

I grr-ed internally. Had Lainey been withholding the paperwork from Cori all this time? I wondered.

"I think that is mainly my fault," I said. "Cori and Lainey are not friends anymore because of me."

"Lainey and Cori are no longer friends as well?" Mrs. Chamberlain asked. She pulled over a stool from her work-table and sat down. "Oh. I never thought—"

But she didn't finish her sentence. Something about how the smile faded from her lips made me wonder what she was thinking.

"Mrs. Chamberlain, would you mind if I spoke openly?" I asked.

Mrs. Chamberlain looked up at me. She waved a hand

to the other stool at her worktable, indicating for me to sit. "*Oui. Oui,* of course."

I sat down and hooked my foot on the crossbar of the stool.

"Well...sometimes it's really hard to be Lainey's friend." I chose my next words as carefully as I could. "It's like she's angry at everyone or something."

Mrs. Chamberlain blinked a few times, and I was afraid I'd messed things up even more. She'd already said she was still considering Cori for a mentorship. What did I have, a death wish or something?

"Angry? That is perhaps true," Mrs. Chamberlain said quietly. "Ever since we adopted Lainey—"

"Lainey is adopted?" Why didn't I know that? But maybe I had never spent enough time to ask. "I had no idea."

"Oh, yes. Mr. Chamberlain has an unfortunate genetic condition," Mrs. Chamberlain said. "We thought it would be best to open our home to a deserving child overseas instead of trying to have our own. Lainey has been with us since just before we moved to Port Toulouse."

I did the mental math—Lainey was adopted when she was in fourth grade? Had she been in foster care before that? An orphanage? It didn't feel right to ask.

"Since we moved here from Europe," she continued, "Lainey seemed to fare well. She has always been so strong—*très independente.* So, we go on as before! Mr. Chamberlain throws himself into his work and charities, and I am consumed with my designs. But perhaps she is not as strong as she lets on? I fear we may have let her down now that I hear she's been so sad."

"I'm sure I haven't helped the situation," I replied.

Mrs. Chamberlain reached out and squeezed my hand.

We both sat silently. I wasn't sure what to say. Had I been so wrapped up in my own stuff that I'd never bothered to find out that Lainey Chamberlain was adopted?

"I think we're all just trying to do our best," I added. "Then someone comes along to show us how we could do better."

"And I think you are not lacking in sparkle, *chère* Jade." Mrs. Chamberlain stood from her stool and smiled. "Tell *Mademoiselle* Blake I would love to be her mentor."

"Really?" I jumped up from my stool. "But would you mind telling her yourself? I think it would mean much more coming from you."

"*Absoluement*," Mrs. Chamberlain replied.

Chapter Eight

GETTING SERENA INTO A bathing suit for our first underwater hockey practice was like trying to slip a tank top onto an octopus. She wanted nothing to do with it.

"Come on, Serena," I whispered, holding out the Speedo Mom had picked out for her at Sport Mart, while the rest of the team got ready in the dressing room. "You're the one who wanted to join the team in the first place. You need to put this thing on."

"Swim clothes without," Serena kept saying.

Devon and Ella from eleventh grade looked over from the other end of the dressing room. Devon was probably our strongest swimmer, considering she was also on the regular swim team. Ella was on the basketball team. They had probably cringed when they saw my name on the sign-up sheet because I was definitely *not* the sporty type. They glanced at each other as if wondering if they'd heard Serena correctly.

"The swimsuits in Tonganesia are just a little different,"

I said, waving off Serena's protests. "I think they use bamboo fibers instead of Lycra or something."

"Oh, I wonder if that's a new thing," Ella said as she tucked her long blond hair under her bathing cap. "That team we're playing next week has those new sharkskin suits like they use in the Olympics."

"They also have Georgia Frum," Devon reminded her. "Remember how she almost drowned Marcelle last year?"

"Don't remind me." Marcelle was a pretty brunette with a cute laugh from tenth grade. She rubbed her throat as if remembering a particularly bad memory. "My food tasted like chlorine for three days after that game."

"Yeah, they beat us every single game last year," Ella replied. "We're going to need some sort of secret weapon if we want to stand a chance against those guys."

"Okay, ladies," Coach Laurena called from the door leading out to the pool deck. "Let's hustle it up in there."

"Do you want us to wait for you?" our other teammate, Charlotte, asked as she tucked her fuchsia-streaked hair behind her multi-earringed ear. She was in tenth grade with Marcelle. In fact, Serena and I were the only ninth graders on the team.

"No, no, you guys go ahead." I smiled and waved them onward. "Just let Coach Laurena know we'll be there in a sec."

It was only Thursday, but I visualized sending Serena back a day early for her weekend with her parents in Talisman Lake if she didn't cut it out with this bathing-suit thing. In only her first week of school, Serena had managed to almost set the science lab on fire with a Bunsen burner, delete our Social Studies project from my hard drive so we had to start all over, and get us both called into the office to be told that shoes were mandatory in school.

"But, house inside. No shoes?" she'd asked when we'd left the office.

I had to sit her down on the bench outside the office for a full ten minutes to explain that yes, we took off our shoes at the house but that the school was not a house. We finally agreed Serena could wear flip-flops instead of shoes except for gym and science class (lab rules), but I wasn't sure how we would explain that once winter hit.

I collapsed into my bed each night, exhausted from constantly having to cover up for her weird ways or explain things for the millionth time.

It was like babysitting six toddlers and a puppy.

Once I heard the door to the pool deck whoosh closed behind Marcelle and Charlotte, I turned to Serena and looked at her sternly. "You've got two minutes to get into your bathing suit and cap, or else I'm quitting this team and taking you with me."

Serena's bottom lip quivered. "No water swim?"

"Only if you put this on." I held the suit out and pointed to the dressing room for her to get changed. If I had to squeeze myself into a Speedo and bare my gleaming white thighs, Serena would have to suck it up and get with the program.

"Everything okay?" Coach Laurena asked as she came in from the pool deck.

"Yeah. Serena's just having a little trouble with the uniform." I looked around to make sure no one else had followed her. Thankfully, Laurena would understand Serena's mer-to-human adjustment period. She was the one who came to our rescue on the barefoot front when she saw us getting pulled into the principal's office.

"Got it." Coach Laurena laughed. "I remember the first time I wore a bathing suit a few years ago. It felt kinda wrong to me, too. Actually, I'm glad I caught you. I was at the diner picking up coffee before work, and Daniel told me Bridget's been having trouble with her legs lately. She keeps saying it's nothing, but do you remember her having trouble walking when you worked at the ice cream parlor this summer? Daniel sounded worried."

I thought back. I knew Bridget had really dry skin on her legs and always carried skin cream around, but I couldn't remember her having trouble walking. "No, I don't think so. But I *did* see her limping the other day. Maybe she twisted her ankle or hurt her knee or something."

"Yeah, maybe you're right."

"Hey, I was wondering." Something had nagged at me since I found out Laurena was a mer. "My mom has never worked or had a driver's license so it hasn't been an issue, but how did you get this job if you're not actually human?" I asked. "And don't you need some sort of birth certificate to get married?"

Which got me thinking. Did that mean Mom and Dad weren't actually married, either? Gah! What if they weren't? Things were certainly getting complicated.

"Well, Eddie got me this job." Coach Laurena laughed. "And I've been engaged for two years now and will probably stay that way for the foreseeable future. Daniel understands, though. It's not such a big deal, I guess."

But something in her eyes suggested otherwise.

"And Bridget?" I asked.

"Eddie's sister's name is Bridget. She lives in Australia now but sent Eddie just enough of her old paperwork for our Bridget to get a driver's license and set up the diner."

"This is all so messed up. I just wish…" I began.

"That things were different? Me, too, kiddo—" but Coach Laurena's words were cut off when she coughed. She pulled out an asthma inhaler from her pocket and coughed a few more times before taking a few puffs. "Oh, excuse me. The air's been really dry around here lately, don't you think?"

"Not really." I looked around the dressing room. The mirrors by the sinks were still steamed up from when the girls took showers before going out to the pool deck.

Coach Laurena put a hand to her chest. "Well, anyway, come on out when you're ready. I'm going to get the girls started on a few underwater drills."

"We'll only be a few more minutes," I assured her as I watched her go.

But something was weird about what had just happened.

I hadn't known Coach Laurena for very long—in fact, she'd only moved to Port Toulouse a few years before—but I couldn't remember her ever using an inhaler before. And Bridget with her limp? Then Luke with all that salt on his fries. And Mom with her new glasses?

Something was definitely up, and I wondered if it had anything to do with the upcoming supermoon.

"Jade! Helping me? Helping me!" The dressing-room door slammed open, and Serena stumbled out. She had her bathing suit on (mostly) except the straps were wrapped around her neck three times and her arms flapped in desperation, trying to get free.

Friday could *not* come soon enough.

Serena and I stepped onto the pool deck with our fins, masks, and snorkels after I rescued her from her wardrobe malfunction. Marcelle, Charlotte, Devon, and Ella were already in the water swimming lengths.

Just remember, I rang to her in my mer voice to make sure none of the other girls could understand. *A few breaths of water and you'll be sprouting a tail again, so use the snorkel like I showed you on that YouTube video.*

Serena nodded. Coach Laurena heard my mer rings and gave us a thumbs-up.

I helped Serena with her diving mask and snorkel, but she fought me like a ten-pound salmon.

"Hold still," I said, snapping her mask strap against my finger hard enough to send a sting through my hand. "Ouch!"

Finally, Serena stood still long enough to get the mask on. She actually looked exactly like everyone else once she had the whole ensemble together. Nobody would have guessed that she secretly lived as a mermaid in Talisman Lake. My confidence about whether this whole plan could work grew. Maybe we could pull this off after all. For now, Serena was just a regular high-school kid from Port Toulouse Regional High.

Well, until she and the rest of us got dragged back to sea in exactly seven days.

I got my snorkel and mask on while Coach Laurena and Serena rifled through the equipment bag full of small handheld hockey sticks and pucks.

"So, since you two are new, I'll explain the basics and you'll get to learn more when we play one on one later," Coach Laurena said.

"Sounds good. But fair warning? I'm not really the sporty type," I warned her. "Last time I played any kind of organized sport, I nearly gave myself a concussion with a badminton racket."

"Well, hopefully this will turn out better for you." Coach Laurena laughed. "Underwater hockey is like ice hockey, but there's a lot less body-checking involved, so it's safer."

"And a lot wetter, apparently," I jumped back as Devon dove in and splashed me.

"Basically, two teams fight for control of a puck at the bottom of the pool," Coach Laurena continued and held up a small stick. "You move the puck around with one of these handheld sticks. The object of the game is to pass the puck to your teammates until you score a goal in the opponent's net."

"Sounds complicated," I muttered. I had trouble keeping up with the rules of table tennis, so this was not a surprise to me.

"You'll get the hang of it. Don't worry." Once Coach Laurena explained the rest of the equipment to us, she stood and blew her whistle.

"Okay, team! We have our first match against IMDH next week so we don't have much practice time. Let's make the most of it," Coach Laurena called out. "Get a few more laps in to get warmed up, and then we'll get right into some shooting and skills."

I walked over to the side of the pool and tested the water with my hand. "Geesh, don't they heat this thing? It's colder than the Atlantic Ocean."

I turned to Serena but she'd already dived in and was three quarters of the way across the pool, underwater, without having to take a single breath.

"Holy-moley," Marcelle said. Charlotte blinked.

Devon and Ella hung to the edge of the pool, staring as Serena flip-turned and swam back to our end. She popped her head out of the water, a huge grin around the mouthpiece of her snorkel. Ella nudged Devon.

"I think we just found our secret weapon."

Chapter Nine

I SAT BESIDE LUKE AS he strummed on his guitar, and watched the glowing embers of the campfire crackle and float off into the early autumn sky. Gran had invited us all to hang out at her cottage on Friday night before Serena dove back into Talisman Lake to spend the weekend with her parents, Finalin and Medora.

"LOL means 'laughing out loud,'" I explained to Serena. She'd wanted to text Chelse as soon as she saw the Beckers' cottage on a nearby island. Serena had mastered smiley faces with a little help from me and Cori and had even made up a mermaidy one for her signature, but she was still having trouble with acronyms. And autocorrect, apparently.

I glanced at her messages back and forth with Chelse.

O<~~{: wish u be here :) :) :) :)
live2text: me toooo!
O<~~{: we do camp fare
O<~~{: camp fear
O<~~{: camp FIRE!

live2text: sounds scary haha LOL

Meanwhile, Trey was entertaining us with his marshmallow-roasting skills before Serena had to go.

"It's just like driving a car," Trey said as he turned the marshmallow at the end of his stick. "Too much gas and you peel out and burn rubber. Too little and you lose traction on the turns."

"Like you would know," Luke teased.

"I'm telling you! There's a fine art to marshmallow roasting," Trey replied. "Oh! Ah!" Just then, his marshmallow caught on fire and he hopped around trying to blow it out.

"You guys told Serena you had a surprise for her. Nobody said anything about burning her lips off," Cori joked as she munched on a graham cracker.

"Here, Serena." Luke put his guitar aside and motioned to the bag of junk food between us. "Toss me a couple of those, and I'll show you how it's really done."

"The mish-minnows?" Serena asked, holding up the bag.

"Oh, but these are far more than just lowly marshmallows," Luke said mysteriously. He attached a few to his stick and turned them over the campfire until they were golden brown on all sides. "Add graham crackers, chocolate, and peanut butter, and you get the ultimate campfire experience—the s'more!"

"Mish-minnow s'mores?" Serena asked.

"Exactly," Luke replied. "But, I invented *this* particular version of s'more in honor of our good buddy Reese."

"Reese!" Serena's face lit up.

I smiled at Luke, and he smiled back. There had definitely been a love connection between Serena and Reese the last time we were all underwater. I couldn't help thinking how sweet it was of Luke to help Serena celebrate her first week of high school in this way.

"Are those Reese's Peanut Butter Cups?" I spied the familiar orange wrapper in the bag. I loved Reese's Peanut Butter Cups almost as much as I loved chocolate-covered WigWags. I showed Serena how to put one on a graham cracker.

"Yup!" Luke laughed. He took the roasted marshmallows and placed them on our s'mores, and then he made another one for himself. Cori and Trey did the same.

The warm marshmallow melted the chocolate and peanut butter, and they oozed out from between my graham crackers as I squished them together.

"To Reese!" Luke held up his s'more in a toast.

"To Reese!" we replied. I bit into the ooey-gooey s'more and went to my happy place.

"Omigarmmm…that is delicious," I mumbled.

"I know, right?" Luke asked, wiping the corner of my mouth with his finger. "What do you think, Serena?"

"I love mish-minnow s'mores!" she said between bites.

Just then, I caught a splash over the lake out of the corner of my eye.

"Wow, the bass are really jumping tonight, huh?" Trey said.

"I don't think those are bass," Luke replied.

And from the sound of the screeching mer rings coming from the middle of the lake, I was pretty sure they weren't bass either.

Once Serena had rejoined her parents underwater, we all sat on the beach in the moonlight while the campfire died out and waited for our parents to come pick us up.

"It's been quite a week, huh?" Luke nudged my shoulder and kissed me on the cheek as he kept strumming his guitar.

"No kidding." Actually, I couldn't believe it had only been a week so far.

Since Serena had arrived, I'd found out that Bridget and Coach Laurena were mers too, and that the Mermish Council planned to force us all back to the ocean with Tidal Law. I'd also joined the underwater hockey team, helped launched an election campaign, and discovered I was expected to ask a boy to a formal dance and dress up in some uncomfortable frilly, taffeta torture device. But I wasn't quite ready to broach the subject of the Fall Folly dance with Luke just yet.

"At least the Jet Skis and boats of Talisman Lake are safe for another week," I muttered.

"Oh. And the humans!" Cori wrapped her hoodie around her shoulders to keep out the evening chill. She and Trey got up and walked to the end of Gran's dock to put their feet in the water.

"But we're no further ahead on that other mer problem," I said to Luke as we sat alone at the campfire.

"There *have* been a few developments," Luke said.

"What kind of developments?" I asked.

"I saw Grandpa at Bridget's this afternoon. He said he had to let a boat through on Wednesday so all those mer prisoners waiting in the canal are now in the lake," Luke replied. "He felt really bad."

"I agree it's sad, but is it really Eddie's problem? Or ours?" I knew that sounded horrible of me, but I was getting tired of the underwater mer world messing up my above-water life. "We're humans now, not mers."

"That might be a totally different story by Thursday," Luke said quietly as he kept strumming his guitar. It was true. The only difference between us and them was the upcoming supermoon.

"So what about Uncle Alzear? Or Reese?" I asked. "Can't they help somehow?"

"Unfortunately, Grandpa says Alzear was one of the prisoners," Luke replied.

"Oh." It felt different now that I actually knew one of the new Freshies.

"And speaking of Reese," Luke nodded to one of the peanut-butter-cup wrappers, "Bridget says she hasn't seen him since earlier this week."

Right. Reese—another friend who was at the mercy of the Mermish Council. Now I felt like an even bigger jerk.

"So now we have no way of knowing what's going on?" I asked. "We're worse off than before."

"Bridget thinks Reese might not be able to get away during

the day or something," Luke said. "She's going to camp out at the beach this weekend to see if she can catch him."

"I still can't believe Bridget is Reese's mom." I folded Serena's clothes and stuffed them in my backpack. "I just don't get how she could have left him behind in the ocean like that."

"It's not like she had much of a choice to take him with her. It's the Mermish Council that decides who get to be Webbed Ones. They control everything." Luke stopped strumming his guitar. "And if Bridget would have stayed in the ocean, Reese wouldn't even *have* a mom."

"What do you mean?" I asked.

"Reese told me once that Bridget was born with a tail defect called scaliosis," Luke said as he put his guitar back in its case. "It got worse and worse as Bridget got older until she couldn't swim at all by the time he was born."

"And not being able to swim is like a death sentence to a mer," I said, feeling really bad for judging her in the first place. "Which is why the Mermish Council let her be a Webbed One."

At the rate I was going, I definitely wasn't going to win an empathy award at my school's next *Character Counts!* assembly.

"And which is why it's probably a good idea that Bridget never becomes a mermaid again," Luke added quietly as he poked the campfire's embers with a stick.

"Wow. I feel like a jerk. I really didn't mean—"

"I know you didn't." Luke smiled and took my hand. "This whole mer stuff is messed up."

"You're not kidding." I thought back to Reese and how he carried Bridget's ID card in his satchel. Sure, it sounded like they kept in contact at Port Toulouse Beach, but stealing a few minutes together with Reese in the water and Bridget on shore was nothing like having my mom finally home with me, sleeping under the same roof. Now Reese might get his mother back if Tidal Law was put into effect, but for how long?

"Hallo!" Dad called out. He and Mom had arrived to pick me up. They walked down the hill from Gran's cottage and joined us on the beach. Dad spotted Luke holding my hand. He did this choking, squawking noise and his eyes bugged out like he was having an allergic reaction.

"Don't take it personally," I whispered to Luke. "My dad thinks I should only start dating *after* I'm married."

"Got it." Luke laughed and waved. "Hello, Mr. and Mrs. Baxter."

"Hello, Luke." Dad spoke slowly and kept staring at Luke, then me, then our entwined hands.

Luke squirmed. "Um, I think I'll go get a bucketful of water to put out this fire." He excused himself and headed to the edge of the shore.

"Oh, Dalrymple." Mom gave Dad a whack on the arm.

"What?" Dad asked, looking innocent. "All I said was 'hello.'"

"And practically vaporized him with your death stare," I said.

"Well, anyway," Mom turned to me, "I hope you kids had fun. Did Serena get away all right?"

"Yep," I replied. "She dove in a little while ago, so she's back in the watery pool of despair with her charming mother and father."

Mom laughed. "Believe me, Serena could do a lot worse for parents than Finalin and Medora."

I stared at Mom, not believing what she was saying. "How can you say that after everything those guys did to you?"

"I'm just saying that as far as parents go…" Mom began but then waved her hand as if to swat the words away. "Oh forget it—don't mind me."

"So, anyway," Dad gave me a quick peck on the cheek and stole a leftover marshmallow from the bag. "Sorry we're late, but I had to make a few pit stops along the way."

Dad popped the marshmallow in his mouth with a mischievous smile.

"Why do I get the feeling one of those stops was to Home Depot?" I joked.

"You know me so well," he replied, wiping his marshmallow-y hand on his shirt. "Actually, I'm glad you guys are all still here. I could use some help unloading the truck."

I was beyond itchy by the time we'd unloaded all the sheets of foil-lined pink insulation into Gran's small den off the kitchen. Mr. Martin had picked up Luke, Trey, and Cori by then, so I was left on my own to help Dad with whatever half-baked plan he had in mind.

"What's this stuff made of, anyway? Itty-bitty

machete-wielding demons?" I shook my arms, trying to free myself of the prickly fibers along my skin.

"Just some foil-lined R4 fiberglass insulation," Dad said.

"Oh, that's good, Dally," Gran said, "because this room can get a bit drafty when the wind is coming off the lake. Could you fix the seal on the windows, too?"

"Sorry, Mom," Dad said to Gran. "This isn't to insulate your den, but I'll get to those windows before the winter, okay?"

"I'm holding you to that." Gran slapped his shoulder a few times on her way back to the kitchen. "There's a Hungry Man turkey dinner in it for you if you get it done by Thanksgiving."

"So what is this stuff *for* then?" I asked, surveying the piles of pink insulation.

"This doesn't have anything to do with Tidal Law, does it?" Mom asked, coming into the room with the toolbox from the truck. "I thought we agreed there was no scientific solution this time."

"There is *always* a scientific solution," Dad said as he flicked open the latch of his toolbox and waved a screwdriver in the air. "Did Archimedes's wife doubt him when he solved the mystery of water displacement while taking a bath? Did Newton's wife debate his theory of gravity when he got bonked by an apple?"

"But Mom isn't exactly your *wife*, now is she?" The words slipped out of my mouth before I could stop them, but my conversation with Coach Laurena had obviously been weighing on my mind.

Mom and Dad stopped what they were doing. They glanced quickly at each other, then back to me.

"No," Dad began. "She isn't, but—"

"Let me." Mom put a hand up to stop him, then took my hand and led me to the couch to sit down. "I guess you figured that out, huh?"

"Took me long enough," I joked.

"Are you okay?" Mom asked. "Because being married or not has nothing to do with how we feel about you. You get that, don't you?"

"I'm okay, but does it bother you guys? Not being married?"

Dad cleared his throat. "I would marry your mom a million times if I could."

"Aw." Mom stood and kissed Dad on the cheek. "And I would say 'I do' a million times in return."

"Oh, gag!" I cried. I guess Mom and Dad were annoying enough as it was, married or not. But, still…

"But since I don't exist on paper," Mom continued, "you're just going to have to keep on *pretending* to listen to your wife."

"Well, you'll be happy to know, I *did* take your advice and decided the wind tunnel at my work would be too obvious and might raise a few questions," Dad replied.

"So you decided to build us a padded room at Gran's house instead?" I asked, looking at the three-inch-thick rectangular slabs of insulation stacked on the floor. "We're mers, not crazy people. Though, I'm wondering about your mental health right now."

"Well," Dad pulled out his measuring tape and sized up the far wall, "some say there's a fine line between genius and insanity, but in this case I think I've come up with a very inspired solution to our supermoon problem."

"Which is—to keep us toasty warm in Gran's den?" I joked.

"Well, it's the aluminum foil layer I need. The insulation part is just to give the foil a bit of structure," Dad said. "It's the best I could come up with at Home Depot. Here, help me with this."

Dad lined up several slabs of insulation on the floor, foil up, so their edges matched. Then he taped them together with metallic duct tape.

"What we're going to do is line this whole room with a foil layer and create a magnetic-free zone for all of you to hide in so that you can escape the magnetic properties of the moon. It's based on the scientific principles of the Faraday cage."

"The Faraday cage?" I asked. "Isn't that the experiment where the cat's in a box and nobody knows if it's alive or dead? Because I don't think that worked out so well for the cat."

"No, that's Schrödinger's box. A Faraday cage is an enclosure that blocks out external electromagnetic fields." Dad pulled the couch to the middle of the room and propped up his patched-together sheets of insulation against the wall. "They're used to protect sensitive computer equipment from lightning strikes and power surges. Hand me another one of those."

I picked up another slab of insulation for Dad while Mom watched with a concerned look on her face.

"I'm really not sure this is going to work, Dal," Mom said.

"My theory is that if a Faraday cage can deflect something as powerful as a lightning bolt, it might just do the trick against a supermoon," Dad said cheerily.

"I just don't want you to get your hopes up." Mom put a hand on Dad's shoulder as he worked.

"Well, apart from three new rolls of duct tape, the only thing I have left is hope," Dad whispered. He pulled off another strip of foil duct tape and fastened two more slabs together without looking our way.

Chapter Ten

WE SPENT MOST OF the weekend remodeling Gran's den into a foil-lined looney bin.

Despite the use of Gran's rubber dishwashing gloves, my forearms were raw from the fiberglass insulation, and by Monday morning I looked like I had scratched them to bits with a metal rake.

"What's that smell?" Cori asked as we walked to school with Serena after popping into Mug Glug's for our Monday morning hot chocolates.

"Some aloe vera cream Bridget gave me," I muttered, trying not to scratch. I'd gone to check on Bridget at the diner the day before. I felt bad about judging her for "abandoning" Reese. We had a good chat, but unfortunately, she hadn't seen Reese over the weekend. "She uses it for her legs and thought it might help, but all I want to do is rip my arms off."

"I noticed she was limping last week," Cori said.

"Bridget is okay?" Serena asked.

"Not really. She thinks it might be her scaliosis acting

up from when she was a mer. Everybody seems off these days," I replied, taking another sip of hot chocolate. "My mom's eyesight is getting really bad, Luke keeps knocking back packets of salt, and Coach Laurena's asthma is really acting up."

"How are you guys feeling?" Cori asked Serena and me as we walked along Main Street.

"Goodly!" Serena replied. Actually, she seemed to have an extra flick in her flip-flops that morning.

"And other than being sleep deprived, I feel completely normal," I added. Every night, the moonlight was getting brighter and brighter through my bedroom window, plus a weird bonging noise from somewhere in the neighborhood was keeping me awake, so I was beginning to feel like a zombie.

"Hopefully everyone will return to normal once we get through the supermoon on Thursday," Cori said.

"*If* we get through the supermoon," I said. "We actually caught my mom sleepwalking around the yard last night."

Once we got Mom back inside, she said the bonging reminded her of the sound mers used in their nurseries to train the mer-babies to sleep and eat. Dad couldn't hear the noise, but he said something about Pavlov's dog, which brought us back to the subject of Schrödinger's cat, then a tense conversation about the Faraday cage, so we all dropped it.

"Dundee that way, right?" Serena pointed northward as we crossed the bridge at the canal.

"Yes," I replied. "You can get there by boat or by car like we did last night coming back from Gran's, remember?"

"Yes." Serena nodded and smiled. She'd obviously been paying attention when Gran showed her where everything was on the map at the school office. She snuck in one last peek at the lake before we stepped off the bridge and headed along Main Street toward the school a mile or so away.

"So…" I snuck a peek at Cori between sips. I had been dying to ask her if Mrs. Chamberlain called to tell her about her mentorship, but Cori hadn't said a word. "Anything new?"

"Not really," Cori replied.

"Anybody call?" I asked.

"No, why?" She narrowed her eyes at me.

I just couldn't help myself; I *had* to know.

"I was just wondering if you heard anything about your mentorship."

Cori looked at me skeptically, then a flash of anger crossed her face. "You were at the mall last week. Did you say something to Mrs. Chamberlain?"

Busted. "Maybe?"

"Ugh. Jade! Why would you *do* that?" Cori shook her head and walked quickly ahead of me.

"Cori, wait!" I called after her.

"Whether or not Mrs. Chamberlain wants to mentor me should be *her* decision." Cori stopped and turned to face me while Serena looked on, confused. "You can't just swoop in and save everyone, Jade. It doesn't work like that in the *real* world."

"That's not what I was trying to do—" How could I explain to Cori that I did it because I felt responsible for screwing things up in the first place? It was my fault for dragging Cori in on the plan to stop Chamberlain Construction from landfilling the tidal pool where my mom was transforming into a human. It was my fault Lainey had it in for Cori. Everything was my fault.

"Well, whatever. Mrs. Chamberlain hasn't called," Cori said sternly, walking onward.

"It's still early. The mentorships don't start until November," I said, following her and hoping she wouldn't stay mad for too long.

"I'm starting to think I'm not cut out to be a fashion designer anyway," Cori said quietly.

"Don't say that. Your designs are amazing," I replied. "Better than anything *I* could ever come up with."

Cori shook her head in irritation.

"And what about you, huh?" she asked. "Have you made any plans?"

"No." It was true. I hadn't given any thought at all to what I'd wanted to do for my school mentorship. The past few months had been so focused on Mom and all the mermaidy stuff happening. But what about me? What was it that I truly wanted? I wasn't sure.

"Well, how about if you worry about your mentorship and I'll worry about mine."

"I'm sorry—" I began.

"No, I'm sorry. Whatever. Just forget it."

But I could tell Cori was still peeved.

Should I not have butted in? Was Cori right? Did I think I could just sweep in and fix everything when *I* didn't even have my act together?

The three of us walked in silence until we reached the bank and I could hear Luke's skateboard as he swerved down Queen Street. He appeared at the corner of Queen and Main and flipped his board into one hand, adjusting the canvas guitar case slung across his chest with the other. We held onto our hot chocolates and jogged up to meet him.

"Hey, guys. Hi, you." He reached for my free hand and gave me a kiss on the cheek, making my heart race. Though my thumping heart might have been from running twenty feet down the sidewalk, something I usually avoided at all costs.

"Where's Trey?" Cori asked, looking over Luke's shoulder. Luke and Trey usually hitched a ride with their mom to her work at the flower shop on Queen Street and then skateboarded the rest of the way together.

"He went with my dad to take his driving test," Luke said as he fell into step with us on the way to school. "Again."

"Just imagine," Cori joked. "By midday there could be one more student driver terrorizing the streets of Port Toulouse."

"Yeah," Luke agreed. "So lock up your pets and look twice before crossing the street!"

"Thankfully, we'll only have one Martin boy to worry about," I teased. "I can't imagine what it will be like when both of you have your licenses."

"What do you mean?" Luke gave me a wry smile and dropped his skateboard to the sidewalk, squeezing my hand before pushing away with three strong strides. "I think I would make an excellent driver—" But a crack in the pavement made him stumble forward and he almost wiped out.

Cori and I laughed out loud.

"Sorry!" I called out, trying to stop laughing. "But you gotta admit—that was pretty funny."

Serena, on the other hand, looked horrified over Luke's stumble. She ran to his side and offered her hand to steady him.

"Luke okay?" she cried, her voice high pitched and strained.

"Yeah, I'm okay." Luke smiled his curvy-lipped, trying-not-to-smile smile and took the hand Serena offered but helped her onto his skateboard instead. He looked at us and gave us a scathing look. "Now at least I know who my real friends are. So *she* gets a free ride to the corner."

"Oh, I'm so jealous," I joked, admiring how sweet Luke was with Serena as he showed her how to hang onto the loop of his backpack so he could tow her along the sidewalk. It reminded me of the time I'd used the Beckers' canoe to tow Mom from Gran's cottage to the bridge so I could get her back to the ocean.

Serena wobbled on the board and grinned a huge smile. "Skate rolling!"

"Go, Serena!" Cori laughed.

"Woo-hoo!" I called, rushing after them. It felt good being just normal teenagers goofing off on a normal day. For a few minutes, I actually forgot that in three days we'd be facing Tidal Law and might be pulled to the bottom of the ocean.

"So, what else is new?" I asked as Cori and I caught up with Luke. We tossed our empty hot chocolate cups into the garbage.

"I heard another boat went missing close to here." Luke steered Serena around the garbage can. "The Howsers' canoe?"

"The Howsers who live by the point close to the bridge?" Cori asked.

Mr. and Mrs. Howser came into the ice cream parlor at least once a week over the summer and shared a sundae on the park bench outside the diner.

"Yeah, that's what they said at the flower shop when I was helping my mom pack a few orders into her van," Luke replied. "Mrs. Howser had left the canoe at the edge of the water on the beach below their house and someone took it overnight."

"Are you kidding me?" I whispered to Luke. I glanced back at Serena but she was too busy concentrating on keeping her balance on the skateboard. I nudged Cori. "I bet Finalin's behind this."

What the heck were Finalin and Medora trying to prove with that stunt? Gran had said the couple would stop vandalizing the boats on the lake (or worse) if we took Serena during the week to give her a "real teenage girl" experience. Had I spent a week mer-sitting her, practically drowning at underwater hockey practice, and dealing with Lainey Chamberlain's wrath over the school election for nothing?

I couldn't say all that out loud, though. Not with Serena there. She couldn't help it that her parents were ungrateful troublemakers.

"I dunno," Luke said. "There might be another explanation."

"Yeah," Cori agreed. "It could be just a coincidence."

"Coincidence, my foot," I muttered.

Luke slowed down when we got to a red light at the corner and steadied Serena so she could get off the skateboard.

"So, new best friend," he asked, "how was your week-end with your mom and dad?"

"Weekend was right," Serena said, though a strange look passed over her eyes as though she felt guilty for having fun on land just then. "I told about election for Mother and Father. And maps. And Folly Dance, too."

I cringed and snuck a peek at Cori. Serena's English was getting a lot better, and that wasn't always a good thing. I still hadn't officially asked Luke to go to the Fall Folly dance because I hadn't had a chance to figure out what I could possibly wear. I'd looked in my closet the night before, but the fanciest thing I had was a pair of jeans I'd bejeweled with Cori during one of our sleepovers last winter.

"Folly dance?" Luke asked. "Oh, that's the thing you and Trey are going to, right?" he asked Cori.

"Yeah." Cori nodded. "The Fall Folly."

"Jade go with Luke!" Serena said enthusiastically.

"Serena…" I muttered, then turned to Luke, trying to act casual. "It's this thing where the girls need to ask the guys to go or something."

"When is it?" Luke asked.

"The nineteenth," Cori replied brightly.

I made a mental note to kill Cori later.

"Of October or September?" he asked.

"September, which I guess is after the supermoon so we shouldn't *really* be making plans beyond Tidal Law, considering," I babbled. "Although October nineteenth has kind of a ring to it. Why does that date sound familiar?"

"Seriously?" Luke got a weird look on his face, making me wonder what was going through his mind. What if he actually didn't want to go to the dance with me?

I glanced at Cori, and an awkward silence fell over our group. Luckily, the light changed and we were off again.

Dodged another bullet.

Thankfully, Cori took Serena to Junior Environmentalists Club during Monday lunch so I didn't have to listen to Cori chew me out for messing up a perfect opportunity to invite Luke to the Fall Folly dance.

The whole conversation had turned out to be so confusing and weird that I wasn't sure I could bring it up again with Luke anyway. Had I sort of invited him? Not really. Had he kind of accepted? I wasn't sure.

So basically, I had no idea if I had a date, needed a dress, or was going to the dance at all.

I took advantage of the Serena break by researching some final details for our joint Social Studies project without the risk of her deleting it on us again. Mom and Dad had been hovering around me since school started, making sure I was finishing my homework so I wouldn't have a repeat performance of last semester, so I really didn't want to mess up on my very first assignment. I was at the library computers, caught up in a Google and Wikipedia time warp, when I heard the "toc, toc, toc" of Lainey Chamberlain's inappropriate shoes winding their way through the aisles of library shelves.

I sank low in my seat and peeked over my monitor. I hadn't really spoken to Lainey since going to her mother's boutique the week before. Sure, I got why Lainey was always so angry, considering everything she had to deal with at home, but I couldn't get over the fact that Lainey hadn't let Cori know that Mrs. Chamberlain wanted to do the mentorship with her. How could I be friends with someone like that?

Thankfully, Lainey didn't notice me as she sat with her back turned at another computer a few rows over, flanked by her entourage.

"There's just something not right about that girl," Lainey muttered. Her nails click-clacked on the keyboard as she chattered with her friends. "She shows up here like she owns the place, and everybody falls all over her like she's some kind of celebrity."

Well, she definitely wasn't talking about me, though I had a feeling Lainey's little rant had something to do with Serena.

"And why does she even *get* to run for class president? She's not even registered for this school. I went to Principal Reamer to lodge a formal complaint but she said that since her registration was still pending, she was allowed," Lainey continued. "How is that fair?"

Yup. Definitely Serena.

"Don't worry," Lainey's friend said. "I asked around and everybody says they're voting for you."

"Well, that's not the point," Lainey said. "She's not even *from* here. She's from some weird tropical place I've never even heard of."

Never heard of it because I wasn't exactly sure if Tonganesia was a real place. What if Lainey found that out? What if she used it against us? What if we were forced to send Serena back to Talisman Lake, and Finalin got ticked off and kept sabotaging boats or worse? He'd pulled Mom underwater while she swam in the lake last summer. What was keeping him from doing it again?

"Oh!" I heard Lainey exclaim as she focused on something from her screen. "That's interesting…"

Oh-oh. That didn't sound good.

Chapter Eleven

I N IT TO WIN it. Dive, dive, dive! In it to win it. High, high, five!"

Things were still a little awkward with Cori after our mentorship talk, but she'd come out for our first underwater hockey game and made up a catchy cheer. She had all the fans in the stands joining in and high-fiving each other as Serena and I stepped onto the pool deck with the rest of our team.

When I say "all the fans," I mean Cori, Luke, Trey, Gran, Tanti Natasha/Mom, and about a half-dozen other people. When I say "stands," I really just mean two of the long wooden team benches they used in the school gym during basketball and volleyball games, which Trey and Luke helped carry onto the pool deck. Underwater hockey didn't exactly draw big crowds, especially since the team had only won two games the season before.

The team from IMDH walked onto the pool deck with their fancy unitardy swimsuits and matching swim caps. They looked like they were on the fast track to the Olympics with those get-ups. Meanwhile, I scanned our mismatched outfits and old equipment and wondered if there had been some kind of scheduling mistake. The IMDH girls definitely looked like they were in a whole different league.

"Is this the same team you played last year?" I asked Marcelle under my breath as we slipped into the pool to warm up.

"Yup," Marcelle answered, her usual cheery smile dissolving into a frown. "That's Georgia Frum with the equipment bag."

"The one with the massive feet," Devon said as she dunked underwater to test her mask.

Georgia's Speedo flip-flops clip-clopped across the pool deck, and the sound reverberated through the pool.

"She does have huge feet," I marveled.

"And hands," Marcelle's own hand went automatically up to her throat. Her brown eyes squinted as she looked across the pool at Georgia's large hands gripping the equipment bag.

"In it to win it!" Cori kept chanting. Honestly, I appreciated her enthusiasm but I wasn't so sure we were going to win anything that day. Our practice the week before had started off well enough with Serena outswimming everyone, but she lacked focus.

Coach Laurena had put us on the same team for the three-on-three scrimmage, but Serena kept swimming back and forth underwater and basically ignored the puck, so the other team kept scoring on us.

"Serena," I said, swimming up to her. "Remember, this is a sport, which means we need to try to win."

I'd been wondering all day whether Lainey Chamberlain had uncovered something at the library that would put Serena's school registration at risk. It would help if I could figure out a way to make Serena indispensable to the school just to be on the safe side. Taking one of our teams up in the regional standings would be a good start. She just needed to focus.

"I need you to imagine that the puck is the key to a lock, okay?" I continued as I treaded water. "You need to help the rest of the team get the key to the net to unlock it. Then we score a goal."

"Like lock at canal? To free Freshie friends of Talisman Lake?" Serena asked thoughtfully.

Oooh, I may have hit on something without even realizing it.

"Yeah—if that helps, then yes."

"All right, team. Hustle!" Our captain, Devon, called us to the side of the pool where Coach Laurena was kneeling so she could give us our last-minute pep talk.

"Okay, so remember"—Coach Laurena took a puff from her inhaler before continuing—"keep feeding the puck to Devon, Charlotte, and Serena on offense. Serena, you have the best speed so I'm counting on you to help Jade, Ella, and Marcelle on defense when you can, too. Jade, you hang back and guard our goal like your life depended on it."

The referee's whistle blew and everyone swam to the middle of the pool to take their places for the face-off.

Like my life depended on it? Yeah, I was kind of getting used to that concept.

"In it to win it. Dive, dive, dive! In it to win it. High, high, five!" Cori kept chanting, bless her optimistic little heart.

The rules of underwater hockey were actually pretty simple for anyone who knew anything about sports. Six players per team, one puck, two nets—and stay underwater long enough to pass the puck or score in the opponent's net. Sounds simple enough? Not really. Even though I technically should have been a better swimmer than most of the people on my team, given I was a *mermaid* and everything, that was so far from the truth it was almost a joke.

I spent most of my time coming to the surface to clear my snorkel and catch my breath, while Devon, Ella, Marcelle, Charlotte, and Serena passed the puck back and forth, trying to get it to the other team's net to score a goal. Since underwater hockey wasn't exactly a popular sport, we didn't have any spare players to trade off and had to play the whole game no matter how tired we were.

Oddly, Serena couldn't hold her breath any longer than I could and had to come up for air just as often, but she made up for it with how fast she could swim.

"Go, Serena!" I yelled, whenever we surfaced at the same time.

"Stealing the key!" she yelled once, waving the puck in the air.

"No, no!" I called back. "The puck needs to stay on the *bottom* of the pool!"

So, yeah. We still hadn't worked out all the rules of the game. In fact, we hadn't managed to score an actual goal by halftime and were down by two, but at least we were giving the IMDHers a run for their money, judging by how they were panting for breath while we took our halftime break at the side of the pool.

"Good hustling down there," Coach Laurena said as we climbed out of the water. "They may have gotten a few goals on us but their team is wearing down."

"Yeah," Devon agreed. "Georgia looks like her head is about to pop off."

It was true. Georgia and all her teammates were red-faced and huffing and puffing, just like us, which I guess was a good sign.

"That's a good look for her," Marcelle said.

"This half, I want you to focus on passing," Coach Laurena said, putting a hand to her chest and pausing for a breath. "And we need a little more hustle out there from some of you."

She obviously was talking about me since I was the one spending the most time above water.

"Ella and Marcelle, tighten up the defense, and Jade, hang closer to the net," Coach Laurena said to us as she wrote on a small whiteboard with a dry-erase marker to demonstrate. "Serena, keep the puck on the bottom of the pool and pass to Devon and Charlotte whenever you get a chance so they can get some shots on net."

"Yeah," Devon chimed in. "Let's get a goal on these guys!"

"Remember, this is a game of offense *and* defense," Coach Laurena continued. "Each position is as important as the other."

The whistle blew to start the second half, and we all swam to the middle of the pool to take our places.

Coach Laurena's pep talk about passing the puck must have lit a fire under Serena's tail because the girl was a stick-handling whiz, scooting the puck along the bottom of the pool, passing it to Devon and Charlotte, and assisting with Devon's first goal of the game partway through the second half.

"Yay!" I sputtered as we all came to the surface for the next face-off after Devon's goal.

"Great pass!" Devon high-fived Serena as she swam over to us, while Georgia Frum sulked with her teammates at the edge of the pool.

Our fans on the bench went wild, and I could see Cori, Trey, and Luke jumping up and down and high-fiving each other. I wondered, was this what being part of a team felt like?

With five more minutes left in the half, we dove back down to the bottom of the pool to continue the game. IMDH took possession of the puck right away so I hustled to our end to guard the net, but by the time I got there, I'd run out of breath and had to resurface.

"Dive! Dive! Dive!" Cori chanted.

Through the water, I could see Georgia and her teammates making a drive for our net. I cleared my snorkel and adjusted my mask, then popped back down into the water and swam to the bottom with all my might just as Serena was swimming to the surface mid-field.

IMDH still had control of the puck, but Marcelle was digging in, trying to get possession, while Ella came to help. Marcelle's hair came undone from under her bathing cap and swayed in front of her face, blocking her sight long enough for one of the IMDHers to steal the puck and break away toward me.

She came at me like a nuclear submarine, but thanks to my, ahem, larger size, I was able to block her shot and clear the puck away to my right. I hoped someone from my team was able to grab it because by then my lungs were about to burst and I pushed off the bottom of the pool to resurface.

I smiled around my snorkel as I saw Serena dive past me on a mission for the puck. Georgia Frum was down there, too, trying to gain control of the play, but quick as lightning, Serena slapped the puck away and swam after it as it rolled along the bottom of the pool. We got lucky and caught the IMDH defenders off guard—they were either at the surface or at the wrong end of the pool.

Serena caught up to the puck and looked for someone to pass it to, but she was the most open.

Go! I rang to her as I dove back underwater to take my place on defense.

Passing? Serena rang back to me, then looked for Devon, who was way behind her. *Passing the puck?*

Just go, go! Score! I replied.

Serena looked to the other team's goal and took off, pushing the puck ahead of her as she swam.

One of the IMDH defenders dove down to the bottom just as Serena got to their end, but Serena faked right, then left, leaving the defender in a fizz of bubbles. She flicked the puck into the goal just before the buzzer rang, ending the game.

We all swam back to the surface with such force and enthusiasm that the whole school probably heard our yells.

"Serena! Serena! Serena!" our fans chanted from the stands. Serena's face broke into a huge smile, realizing what she'd done.

"You did it!" I grabbed her around her shoulder as we bobbed in the water. "You tied the game!"

"Key in the lock!" Serena exclaimed.

"Key in the lock," I agreed.

Our underwater hockey season was off to a splashy start.

Chapter Twelve

THURSDAY, SEPTEMBER 17, ARRIVED like a double
final-exam day. Not only was Tidal Law supposed
to take effect tonight, but it was also Election Day, and
the school cafeteria had been turned into a polling station
during lunch hour. Our homeroom teacher had given me
permission to help Serena fill out a ballot, since she'd never
voted before.

"Just put an X in the box of the person you want to vote
for in the different categories." I pointed to the different
sections of the ballot to explain how it worked to Serena.

Serena marked her choices for school president, vice
president, treasurer, and secretary after having heard their
speeches at that morning's general assembly. For the ninth-
grade class rep, though, she hovered her pen over the choices.

☐ Lainey Chamberlain
☐ Serena Finora
☐ Raymond Fresco

After a few moments, she checked the box next to Lainey's name.

"You're voting for Lainey?" I asked, not believing what I'd just seen. "Haven't you noticed she's done nothing but be rude to us?"

"But she hard worked on her signs," Serena said.

I laughed. No wonder so many people liked Serena. There was no way I'd be able to vote for Lainey after how mean she'd been. I still couldn't get over the fact that Lainey hadn't let Cori know about the mentorship, and since Cori hadn't mentioned whether Mrs. Chamberlain had gotten in touch yet, I was having trouble letting that go.

"Okay...if you're sure," I checked off my choices, including Serena's name.

"Serena!" Devon walked over to us with a bunch of other eleventh-grade girls and put an arm around Serena. She addressed her friends. "This is the girl I was talking to you guys about. She helped us finally tie a game against IMDH on Tuesday. You should see her swim!"

"Awesome."

"Cool."

A group of ninth graders looked up from their table and turned our way. As luck would have it, one of them was Lainey Chamberlain.

"Pftt," Lainey said under her breath and rolled her eyes. "Don't get used to it. She's not going to be here for long."

Devon nodded Lainey's way. "What does that girl

mean? You're not moving, are you?" she asked Serena. "You just got here."

"No, no—nothing like that." I shot a glance at Lainey, then turned to Devon. "We're just having a little trouble getting Serena's old school records so she can officially transfer here."

"Well, I hope it all works out," Devon said before she headed to the cafeteria line with her friends. "Because I have a feeling we're going to have a great season. See you at practice!"

"Just a little mix-up," I said to the table of ninth graders. "She's still running for School Council rep, so make sure you vote!"

A few of the girls whispered among themselves. They looked from Lainey to Serena, then went to the voting station to pick up their ballots.

"Mix-up, right." Lainey narrowed her eyes and stood up from the table. Then she stalked off in the direction of the library.

This wasn't good. Not good at all.

Serena took forever to brush through her super-long hair and get dressed after our underwater hockey practice after school. Everyone had pretty much cleared out of the dressing room, yet there I sat, waiting for the aquatic goddess to finish packing all her things in her swim bag. She kept rooting through the bag, arranging and rearranging things.

My cell phone buzzed. It was a text from Dad.

@geeksrule: gran and 'tanti natasha' are on their way. tonite is the nite! faraday to the rescue!

"Will you hurry up?" I asked. It was the night of the supermoon and we were going to put Dad's foil-lined Faraday room to the test. "Gran and Mom are on their way, and Coach Laurena is waiting for us in her office."

If Dad's plan worked, we'd avoid being forced back to the ocean to help the Mermish Council squash the political uprising. If it didn't, me, Luke, Serena, Mom, Bridget, and Coach Laurena could be sleeping in a very soggy bed.

"Flip-floops!" Serena cried, searching in her bag.

Oh, her beloved flip-flops. She'd collected six pair so far and had been wearing them morning, noon, and night since we had the conversation about her going barefoot in school.

"Didn't you have them when you came in?" I searched all the small cubby lockers to see if she'd stashed them in a different spot.

Serena looked at me hopelessly.

"Maybe they're back on the pool deck," I suggested. Honestly, it was like getting a five-year-old ready for kindergarten. "Come on, I'll help you look."

Just then Coach Laurena called out from the rec-center hallway.

"You ladies almost done in there? I need to lock up the dressing rooms."

"Yeah, almost," I called back. "Serena forgot her flip-flops, so I'm helping her look for them."

"I'm just going to get the equipment bag in my trunk for next week's game," Coach Laurena replied. "Come to the office to find me once you're done, okay?"

"Got it," I said.

It was eerily quiet as we stepped onto the pool deck. I kicked off my street shoes by the door. The soles of my feet made a flapping noise that reverberated through the empty space.

"You look over by the diving board, and I'll check by the lane markers." Charlotte and Marcelle were *supposed* to have been in charge of replacing the lane markers after our practice, but they were still lying along the deck at the side of the pool. Sure enough, Serena's flip-flops were hidden underneath.

"Got 'em!" I called out. "Help me get these things back in place, then we can meet Coach Laurena."

The door to the girls' dressing room squeaked open and someone walked onto the pool deck.

"We'll be right there," I called out as I pulled a blue and white lane marker out and over the surface of the water to get the pool ready for lane swimming.

I heard the "toc, toc, toc" of high heels behind me and my stomach cramped. Lainey Chamberlain. What the heck could she possibly want?

"Lane swimming isn't for another hour," I said, turning toward her.

Lainey kept walking toward us, her face set in a determined scowl. "I'm not here for the lane swimming."

"You don't say?" I tried to stay cool. Serena and I

hooked the lane marker in place and crossed the deck to get the next one. Lainey's heel slipped a little, but she kept her balance. "Oh! Be careful there—you're not really supposed to wear shoes on the pool deck."

But Lainey just kept toc-tocking toward us.

"You're the one who should be careful," Lainey said smugly. "Especially considering the circumstances."

Today of all days was not the time to get into it with Lainey Chamberlain. If the Mermish Council got its way, Serena (and the rest of us) would be out of the picture for good anyway. Not that I was planning on that happening.

"I have no idea what you mean, Lainey." I glanced at Serena and then at my watch. It was already past five o'clock. The days were getting shorter, and we needed to get to Gran's cottage before the sun went down because once the supermoon was in full force and Tidal Law took effect, we'd be like sitting ducks.

"Well, I've been doing some digging around," Lainey said. "And you'll never guess what I came up with."

She knows something, Serena rang to me. Her English comprehension was getting quite good. Even she could tell that Lainey was getting ready to go for the kill.

Maybe she's bluffing, I rang back. But Lainey knew something—I just wasn't sure what it was yet.

"If you've got something to say, Lainey, just spit it out," I replied.

"Well, as you know, Serena can't become a student here unless she gets all her school records."

"Wow, that's some really excellent investigative reporting, Lainey." I tugged at the end of another lane marker to get the rope untangled. "Especially since that's the same thing you overheard while I was talking to Ms. Wilma."

"Oh, there's more," Lainey said as she continued to pace along the pool deck.

Serena looked from Lainey to me, trying to follow the conversation as best she could.

Am I in trouble? she asked in her mer voice.

Just play it cool, I rang back.

"There is no possible way of getting her school records," Lainey said, "because the school you claim Serena used to go to doesn't exist."

My insides cramped into a tight ball of agony. Had Lainey actually snooped around to find all this out?

"Furthermore," Lainey continued, "I had Daddy's attorney look into it, and apparently there's no record of a Serena or Natasha Finora traveling into this country for the past six months. So, how exactly did they get here? Seems to me that's a question for the immigration officials." Lainey came to a stop by the remaining lane markers and adjusted her shoulder bag over her shoulder. Her knuckles grew white as she grasped its handles.

"There must be a mistake." I struggled to keep my voice from wavering. "My grandmother is getting all the paperwork straightened out. This will all be taken care of next week."

"We all know that's not true!" Lainey stalked toward me, waving a finger in the air. But before she could make it two steps, her high heel slipped on the wet deck and got caught in the loose rope at the end of the lane marker. She tumbled forward, whacking her head on the side of the pool. Lainey hit the water with a sickening plash and sank to the bottom of the pool in a tangled mess.

What Bridget had said about how ancient mer laws controlled us was true because just then a powerful force took over me. Before I knew it, I dove into the pool after Lainey. Serena did the same, and we both zipped to the bottom. The rope was wrapped around Lainey's neck and arms and had gotten snagged on the hockey goal under water. I tried to set it free from around her neck, but it held tight.

Help me! I rang to Serena, but she was too busy trying to get the rope untangled from the goal.

Lainey's hair swirled around her limp body. I worked the knots, trying to get the rope to loosen so I could free her. We had to save her!

Without thinking, I took a huge gulp of water. The chlorine seared my throat as it burned through to my lungs. It may not have been the Atlantic Ocean, but the water in the pool was enough to set off a familiar big, red panic button inside me.

Before I knew it, a blast of water exploded from my legs, leaving in their place a slippery, icky, very inconvenient tail.

No! I rang, trying to figure out how I was going to explain all this to Lainey Chamberlain once we got her back above water. *If* we got her back above water. Thankfully, keeping humans from drowning worked much better as an actual mer and I swam back to Lainey's side, untangled the rope, and pulled her to safety in a matter of seconds.

"Serena!" I yelled as soon as I surfaced. But Serena was nowhere in sight.

I yanked Lainey over the side of the pool and rolled her onto the pool deck to check her breathing.

She wasn't breathing! I forced a gulp of air down my lungs and tried to remember the steps for artificial respiration from my baby-sitter's course the summer before. I braced my elbows against the pool deck and tilted Lainey's chin back to give her a few breaths before she started coughing.

"Thank god!" I gasped as Lainey turned to her side and hacked out a mouthful of water.

"What…" Lainey held her head where she'd struck it and blinked, trying to make sense of what had just happened.

I was just about to hop out of the water to help her sit up when I remembered—I had a tail! A tail that was starting to burn because it was about to start turning back into legs the more I breathed fresh air. Maybe if I just stayed in the water, Lainey wouldn't notice?

"Omigod! What the heck is that? Omigod!"

Too late.

Lainey shrieked and pointed into the water. She stood slowly and wavered for a second, trying to get her balance. But she wasn't pointing at me—she was pointing at the other mer-girl. Serena. In all her tailish glory.

"Lainey, I can explain—" I started, but the pain shooting up my tail stopped me mid-sentence.

"And you?" Lainey's eyes grew wide. "You, too?"

The door from Coach Laurena's office flew open. She ran out onto the pool deck with Mom and Gran at her heels.

"Jade!" Mom called.

"Mom!" I called back without thinking.

Lainey stared in astonishment at Mom, then me. She backed away from the side of the pool, her hands up to her face as if not trusting what would come out of her mouth. Then she grabbed her bag, turned, and ran to the dressing room, limping along on a lone shoe as she went.

"Lainey, wait!" I cried.

But it was too late. Lainey was gone.

Chapter Thirteen

THANKFULLY, MOM, GRAN, AND Coach Laurena were there to help Serena and me. We could have been ambushed by news crews reporting live within the hour if anyone else had discovered two teenage mermaids swimming around in our small-town community pool.

I could just imagine the *National Enquirer* headlines!

Actually, I was totally surprised no one *had* come looking for us since Lainey Chamberlain had run out of there like a girl on a mission. And, let's be honest, Lainey was always on the lookout for ways to be the center of attention. Making a mer discovery would have definitely boosted her popularity rating on a global scale.

But, nope. Nothing.

"Are you guys okay?" Coach Laurena asked as she returned from her office with a spare pair of gym pants after locking all the doors. Gran and Mom fussed around me as I tried to calm my breathing.

"Yeah, Jadie girl," Gran said, rummaging through her handbag. "Can I get you a tissue or a cough drop or something?"

"I'll be fine, but we need to get Serena out of here." I filled everyone in on what had just happened while I hurried to get dressed.

Hold on, Serena, Mom rang. *I'm calling Jade's dad to get the Merlin 3000 here as soon as possible.*

Serena gazed back up through the water, a desperate look on her face.

"He's heading home to get the trailer right now," Mom said once she hung up.

I texted Trey, Cori, and Luke to be on the lookout for Lainey while Gran kept Serena company until Dad arrived.

Finally, there was a knock on the emergency exit door to the back parking lot.

Gran stood guard as Dad, Mom, Laurena, and I quickly loaded Serena into the Merlin 3000. Then we all piled into Dad's and Gran's vehicles to make the trek to Dundee. Since it was Thursday, Serena decided to return to Talisman Lake a day early for her weekend visitation with her parents, which was just as well, considering Tidal Law was about to close in on us.

That whole pool drama had put us way behind schedule, and by the time the Martins and Cori got to Gran's cottage and we had everyone settled in Dad's Faraday room, it was 7:00 p.m. and getting dark. The bonging noise that I'd been hearing every night for the past week increased with every passing minute. That, combined with what had just happened at the pool, was seriously messing with my head.

"Are you *sure* you didn't see where Lainey went?" I

asked Cori for the millionth time as she sat at a small table in Gran's den with Trey, playing cards with his parents. I flicked through the channels on the small TV perched on the bookshelf in the corner, hoping I wouldn't see a headline with my name on it. "What if she tells somebody what she saw? She could be juggling offers from a dozen different TV networks right now."

"Like I said," Cori said patiently, even though I could tell she was still annoyed with me for talking to Mrs. Chamberlain behind her back, "I was waiting for Trey by the front doors when she blew right by me with one shoe, talking to someone on her cell. I saw her get into one of those black sedans from her dad's company, probably getting picked up by his driver, but that's all I know." She looked at her cards and set them down on the table with a self-satisfied smile. "Rummy."

Just then, Gran called out from the kitchen next to the den.

"Dinner's almost done," she said as she pulled the third foil pan of supermarket lasagna from her old-fashioned gas oven.

"Smells delicious, Gran," Mom said as she brought plates into the den. She bumped into the table and I caught her arm to keep her from falling.

"You okay?" I asked.

Mom blinked. Her eyes were really red and swollen behind her glasses. "Yes, yeah. I'm sorry. I should have brought my eye drops. Everything's just a little blurry."

"Is everybody here?" Gran asked as she set the lasagna on the coffee table. "I wonder if I got enough food."

"It's plenty, Mom." Dad kissed Gran on top of her silver-curled head. "Thanks for going to all the trouble."

"No trouble at all, Dally." She squeezed his cheeks and returned to the kitchen as the phone rang.

"*Is* everyone here?" I wondered aloud.

Four mers: me, Luke, Coach Laurena, and Mom.

Six two-leggers: Cori, Trey, Mr. and Mrs. Martin, Dad, and Gran.

That made ten people crammed into the den like sardines in a tin can. Getting Serena back into the lake had probably been a good idea because space was tight and the room felt like the inside of a toaster oven. Still, we were missing a mer.

"Where's Bridget?" I asked, looking around the room.

Coach Laurena pulled out her phone to check her texts. "Eddie and Daniel are out looking for her right now."

"What do you mean, *looking* for her? Is she missing?" A kernel of worry grew in my belly. Tonight was not the night for a mer to be roaming the streets (or beaches) of Port Toulouse. As soon as the supermoon was in full force, any mer was a moving target.

"Bridget never showed up at the diner this morning," Coach Laurena said. "Daniel knew she'd been camping out at the beach a few nights a week, looking for Reese, so he just figured she'd slept in. By noon, though, she still hadn't showed up. Daniel got worried, so he closed up the diner and has been looking for her ever since."

"This isn't good." I checked my phone, then placed it back on the coffee table and snuck a glance through the den door to the kitchen window. It was still a little light out, but it would be completely dark in half an hour or so. I turned to Dad. "Let's go, too. The more people looking for Bridget, the better."

"No, it's not going to help to have everyone roaming around." Dad looked at me and rubbed his head. "Eddie and Daniel are doing everything they can."

"Here, Jade. Help me with the cutlery." Gran handed me a box of plastic knives and forks.

"Oh, and by the way, Dally, that was Wilma on the phone. She said Principal Reamer needs Serena's records by Monday or else Serena won't be able to keep coming to school for insurance reasons. Any idea when those will magically appear?"

"Your guess is as good as mine." Dad got up and closed the den door, shutting us off from the rest of the house—the rest of the world for that matter—in his foil-lined looney bin.

"I guess that's the least of our worries, huh?" Luke whispered to me. "No use planning anything beyond Tidal Law, isn't that what you said?"

That *was* what I had said during our completely discombobulated Fall Folly conversation. Urg. I smiled weakly.

"Well, then," Gran called out and cut into the steaming lasagna before I could reply. "Let's eat!"

Amazingly, I'd just lost my appetite.

By 8:30 p.m., there was still no word on Bridget. With all the windows covered and the door closed, we had no way to tell how dark it was outside. But the bonging noise reverberating through my body was proof enough that the moon was out in full force.

"I haven't gotten a text from Daniel for half an hour," Coach Laurena said as she rubbed her throat. "Something is wrong."

Luke sat next to me on the couch. We hadn't really talked since his comment about not planning anything past Tidal Law. He'd only picked at his food, but he kept sucking on a piece of garlic bread as if trying to get all the taste out.

"I'll be right back," he said, jumping up. "Just got to get the salt shaker from the kitchen."

"No!" Dad stood by the door to stop him. "Nobody who's ever had a tail gets to leave this room until tomorrow morning."

Coach Laurena pulled out her inhaler, shook it, and took a few puffs.

"Asthma still bothering you?" I asked.

"Yeah," she answered, taking off her sweater. She coughed a few times and cleared her throat. "Wow, it's warm in here, huh?"

"Hotter than hot," I replied, standing up from the couch and crossing the room to see if I could find a pocket of cool air away from the crowd.

"Luke!" Mrs. Martin called from behind me.

I heard a thud and turned. Luke was on the floor, shaking all over.

"What's happening?" I cried, rushing to his side.

"He's been acting strangely for days," his mom said, handing him another piece of garlic toast from the coffee table. He took it in his hands and sucked on it hungrily. "It's like he's hypoglycemic but for salt instead of sugar. I don't know what's going on with him."

Luke's dad came over to help, too, and everyone started tripping over each other, trying to get around in the small space.

Meanwhile, Coach Laurena sat on the couch, her hands braced against her knees. Her breath came out in wheezy gasps, and her eyes were vacant like she was in a trance. That's when I noticed Mom staring over Dad's shoulder, her eyes red and swollen.

"It's Tidal Law," I said under my breath, trying to piece everything together.

"What do you mean?" Dad asked.

I glanced from Luke to Mom to Coach Laurena and could feel them slipping away from us one by one.

"It's affecting everyone differently. Luke with his salt cravings, Laurena with her asthma, and Mom with her eyes," I replied. "I'm just not sure why I don't feel any different."

"Maybe since you weren't born a mer," Cori chimed in.

"But that doesn't explain why Serena—" I began but was interrupted when Luke jumped up and lunged for the door. "He's trying to get out!"

Dad and Mr. Martin grabbed Luke but he flailed against them, trying to break free. Mom and Laurena were next, and soon it was a mer-versus-human struggle to keep Mom, Laurena, and Luke from breaking down the door.

Water! All three of them kept ringing in their mer voices, as if in a trance. Coach Laurena's breathing was completely out of whack, and from what I could see amid the struggle, Mom's eyes had swollen shut, and Luke had resorted to licking people's faces for our salty sweat.

Charming.

Water! they continued.

"I really thought the Faraday room would help, but the force of the moon is too strong," Dad yelled. "They're being compelled to the ocean."

"What are we supposed to do?" I yelled over the commotion. "We can't let them get anywhere near the coast."

Dad and Mr. Martin still had Luke by the arms, but it was getting harder to hold him still. Trey and I grasped Mom, and Mrs. Martin helped Cori hold Coach Laurena back while Gran did her best to clear any furniture hazards.

With seven of us and three of them, we were able to control them, but I wasn't sure for how long.

Seconds after the thought crossed my mind, Luke broke free and grabbed for the door. He escaped and headed outside but not before grabbing the keys to his parents' car from the hallway table.

"Luke, no!" I ran after him and out the door. The sheer size of the supermoon made me stop for a split second at the top of the porch steps. It formed a perfect white circle and gleamed like a huge pearl against a black velvet backdrop.

I heard the car start and the taillights flickered on.

"You've gotta be kidding me!" The car was already rolling down the driveway by the time I reached for the handle of the passenger door. I opened it and launched myself inside.

Ocean! Water!

"Are you out of your mind? The ocean is miles away! And you don't even have a license!" How did he think he was ever going to make it to Port Toulouse without ending up dead in a ditch?

Water! Luke rang.

"I should have thrown you in the lake with Serena when I had the chance!" That's when it hit me.

I grabbed the steering wheel and turned it toward the lake with all my might.

Water! Luke rang even louder than before, struggling against me. But little did he know, I came from very sturdy stock. I elbowed him in the nose and gripped the wheel.

Ow! Water! he repeated.

"Oh, you're going to get water, all right," I said between gritted teeth as I reached my foot over to the driver's side, feeling for the accelerator. I kept manhandling the steering wheel as Luke fought against me. I finally jammed my foot over his to put the pedal to the metal. We careened down the bank toward Gran's dock, and the car launched into the air when we hit the end of the deck.

"Dive! Dive! Dive!" I yelled for the split second we were airborne, which seemed like an appropriate chant for drowning your boyfriend. I found the down button for the passenger side window and waited for impact.

We hit the water in spectacular fashion and sank to the bottom of Talisman Lake.

Chapter Fourteen

O KAY, SO I DIDN'T exactly *drown* Luke, but I hoped that escaping from a car at the bottom of Talisman Lake would take enough time to *kinda* drown Luke—or at least trap him underwater long enough so he could change into a mer-boy.

Are you crazy? Luke rang through the water as he tried to get past me to escape through my open window.

Trust me! Just take a deep breath, I rang back.

I blocked his way and felt a final glub of car air escape around me as it made its way to the surface. Lake water flooded my nostrils and throat.

No, I need ocean *water,* Luke cried in anguish as if I were denying him a drink in a barren desert.

I'll get you to the bridge once you change. There's more salt water there, but at least the lock will keep you from getting dragged into the ocean. I held out my arms and wrestled him into a hug.

Luke fell into my arms and went limp, as if not knowing what else to do. I felt him take a deep breath so I sucked in some lake water, and within seconds the car shuddered with the force of our tail transformations.

Come on. I helped Luke out the open passenger-side window and swam out into the lake, away from the car. The whiteness of the moon shimmered overhead through the water.

Feel better? I asked as we swam away.

That depends on what my mom and dad say once they realize I just drove their car into the lake, Luke replied.

Thankfully, lake water seemed to have taken some of the edge off, and Luke was a little less out of it. Still, with the moon and the bonging noise still in full force, he was jittery and nervous looking and was having trouble catching his breath in the fresh water—the way I felt when I was low on my recommended daily allowance of chocolate-covered WigWags. Okay, so maybe Luke was a little worse off than that.

I'm pretty sure I was the one who elbowed you in the face so I'll take the rap, I rang, spinning around in the water, trying to make sense of which way the cottage was, when I spotted a light off in the distance. *Wait here a sec.*

I took a big breath of water before popping my head out into the night air.

"Jade!" I could hear Dad and Mr. Martin's frantic calls as they stumbled down the hill in the dark. "Luke!"

"I'm okay! We're both okay!" I hollered back. "Bring Mom and Laurena to the dock!"

I dove again to catch my breath underwater and resurfaced.

"And fair warning, you're all about to get very wet!"

It broke my heart into a million pieces, helping Dad hold Mom underwater as she struggled against us while Trey and

Mr. Martin did the same with Laurena. They were both so out of it, crazed by the forces of Tidal Law trying to lure them back in the ocean, that it was impossible to explain what we were trying to do.

Mom flailed her arms and struggled against us as we held her down. Snippets of memory from when Mom disappeared in almost that same spot last year flashed through my mind. I'd cursed Finalin and Medora so many times for forcing Mom underwater against her will and there I was, doing the same thing.

I felt the rush of current from Laurena's transformation first, and a few seconds later, Mom slipped from my grip as she did the same.

I popped my head out to let Dad in on my plan. "The water is way too fresh here, but I'll swim them back to the lock where the water is saltier."

"What should *we* do?" Dad asked frantically. "Should we go to the bridge and meet you there? Maybe the Martins and I should help look for Bridget, and Trey and Cori can stay with Gran."

The moon shone on Dad's wet face, reminding me of the time we'd rescued Mom and Serena from the tidal pool behind Port Toulouse Mall. All Dad had wanted back then was to get his family back on solid ground, and here we were a few weeks later, trapped just like before.

Worse than before.

I took a minute to catch my breath underwater before facing Dad again. But before I could resurface I saw a tailed figure swimming toward us through the dark waters.

Serena? What are you doing back here? I asked. *And why are you crying?*

It was pretty much pandemonium underwater as I tried to figure out what was wrong with Serena while Mom swam blindly underwater now that her glasses were long gone. Coach Laurena continued to wheeze for breath, and Luke still shook like crazy from lack of salt.

"Here!" Cori yelled from the dock, passing me a plastic bag full of water in the moonlight. She'd remembered how the box of salt had helped Luke the last time we rescued him from Talisman Lake. Trey had the bright idea of pouring some of the salt in a bag full of lake water so Luke could breathe in and out of it like the paper bag Coach Higgins had given me the time I overdid it and hyperventilated on Sports Day.

Luke took a few deep breaths from the bag and his whole body seemed to sigh in relief.

"Thanks, Cori. I think it's helping," I said as I handed bags through the water to Mom and Laurena, too.

"Don't mention it," she said, grasping my arm. "Just... well, you know."

I nodded and dove back in. The salt water didn't fix Mom's eyesight or Laurena's breathing, but they could at least think a little more clearly compared to the trance they'd been in back in the cottage.

I took advantage of the break in the action and pulled Serena aside.

So, what happened? I asked. *I thought you'd be with your mom and dad and the rest of the Freshies by the bridge by now.*

I went there, Serena replied in Mermish, *but Mother and Father are gone.*

Gone where? I asked.

They took the Howsers' canoe, just like you suspected, Serena said, *and filled it with salty water from near the bridge. Their plan was to try to swim the whole length of the lake to the northern passage.*

I thought for a second. Finalin probably got the canoe idea from when I transported Mom from Dundee to the locks at the beginning of the summer. But no Freshie had ever been further than Dundee because of the freshness of the water in the middle of the lake. A canoe full of salt water might be their ticket out of there, though.

How do your mom and dad know about Folly's Passage? I asked slowly.

I told them after I saw that map in the school office. Serena looked away as if she'd betrayed a secret. *I told them about the rebellion, too. And about voting and elections and democracy. I should have known that would make Father and Mother want to escape more than ever.*

Finalin was just crazy enough to try to make it to Folly's Passage.

Now Mother and Father are risking their lives to fight the Mermish Council, Serena continued. *All they've ever wanted was freedom for me. For everybody.*

Something shifted inside my head. I thought about Mr.

Chamberlain and how evil I thought he was with all his shady construction deals. Yet he sponsored all those *Safe 2 Swim* events and worked for a ton of charities. I didn't exactly agree with his methods, but deep down, maybe his heart was in the right place.

What if Finalin and Medora weren't totally the bad guys here? Sure, they'd done some pretty nasty things, like vandalizing boats on the lake and pulling Mom underwater last summer, but that was mostly to buy freedom for their daughter and to figure out a way to escape. And what about all the other mers who were imprisoned and whose only crime had been to stand up for themselves against the Mermish Council? Didn't they deserve their freedom?

But was that really my problem? I was a human first and a mer second, wasn't I? Why couldn't I just go back to being a normal teen girl trying to get over her fear of awkward dancing long enough to ask a boy to her first formal?

What if Mother and Father never make it? Serena continued. *What if they end up with Folly, shipwrecked at the bottom of the lake?*

I looked around. At Luke, who was breathing into the bag of salty water and trying to stop from shaking. At Coach Laurena, who was still gasping for breath. At Mom, who kept blinking, trying to clear her vision. The Mermish Council had caused all this.

I popped my head out of the water and called for Gran.

"How far is Folly's Passage compared to the bridge in Port Toulouse?" I asked.

"The bridge is about three miles south, and I'd say the passage is about five or six miles to the north." Gran looked up and down the lake and waved her hand as she spoke. "Why?"

"Just working on a plan," I said before diving again.

Okay, here's what we're going to do. I waved Mom, Laurena, and Luke toward Serena and me and went over my loosey-goosey plan, but the more I talked it out, the clearer it became.

Mom, Laurena, and Luke, I continued, *you guys each take a bag of salt water and swim to the bridge.*

Wait, what are you planning to do? Mom blinked, trying to focus on my face underwater.

I'm going to help Serena find her parents at the other end of the lake.

No, Mom said. *If that's the plan, I think we should stick together and all go north.*

You're kidding, right? I asked. *You can barely see. Laurena can barely breathe, and Luke is shaking like a jackhammer salesman. It will be better if you guys stay safe behind the locks of the bridge.*

But you've never been any farther north than here, Mom said. *What if you get lost?*

I popped my head out of the water.

"Dad, can you guys get the Martins' boat to lead Serena and me to Folly's Passage so she can find her parents?" I asked.

"I guess…" Dad said slowly. "As long as it's okay with your mother."

So it's settled? I asked Mom as I resubmerged.

I see what you did there, Mom said with a wry smile. *Still, though—*

Serena is much more used to fresh water than any of us, and I feel fine, I assured her. *I'll get Dad to load the boat with some more bags of salt water. Trey and Cori will help him.*

Luke took a huge breath of salt water from his bag and looked me straight in the eye. The salt water must have done the trick because his gaze was steady and straight.

I'm coming with you.

Yeah, right, I rang. *We just spent all night trying to keep you from the ocean, and now you want swim right into it?*

Look, Luke said. *I feel fine and it's like I said back at Bridget's Diner: the Mermish Council might force me into the water with all this Tidal Law crap, but there's no way I'm going to become one of their puppets.*

If you're sure, I rang slowly, hoping I wouldn't regret it. *I'm sure,* he replied. *Are you?*

Chapter Fifteen

WE WERE LIKE TWO royal caravans heading off in different directions as Dad, Cori, and Trey accompanied us northward, feeding us bags of salty water through the freshest part of the lake, while Mr. and Mrs. Martin rowed Gran's rowboat to keep an eye on Mom and Coach Laurena on the way to the lock.

Gran decided her talents were of best use on land, so she returned to her cottage to clean up and to call the tow truck to get the Martins' car out of the lake.

The moon still shone brightly and felt like a bare light bulb in an investigation room on one of those TV police dramas Dad watched. Luke struggled for the first few miles, but as we traveled further north, I could feel the lake growing saltier. We swam for another hour or so before the water became shallow and weedy.

It must have been close to midnight by the time I heard the boat's engine whirr to a lower gear.

We must be close, I said to Serena and Luke. *You guys okay?* Serena nodded.

Yes! Luke said in a strong, re-energized ring. His shakes were completely gone, and he swam easily and confidently. Actually, he looked like a mer on a mission, the way he zigged and zagged through the water.

I couldn't help wondering what Luke had meant when he asked me if I was "sure" before we started on our swim up the lake. Was it just about our plan to swim north or some leftover weirdness from almost-but-not-quite asking him to the Fall Folly? Was he wondering if I still wanted to be his girlfriend? Ah! This boyfriend-girlfriend stuff was so complicated.

"Jade?" I heard Dad call from the boat.

"What's going on?" I asked as I popped my head out of the water.

"I think that's the Howsers' canoe washed up on shore." He pointed a high-powered flashlight toward the bank. Sure enough, a canoe was swamped and tilted at an odd angle along the shoreline.

"Can you get this attached so we can tow the canoe out of there?" Dad handed me a rope with a carabiner.

"Hold on a sec."

I swam to the canoe and hooked the carabiner to the canoe's crossbar, then swam out of the way so Dad could haul it out into the open water with the boat's winch. Cori and Trey helped him pull the canoe aboard *The Lady Sea Dragon.*

There's nothing in there, I rang to Serena and Luke as the water drained from the canoe.

Well, at least we know Mother and Father have made it this far, Serena rang through the water, sounding relieved.

What do you want to do? I asked.

We need to keep going! Serena said. *They could be in the ocean by now. We need to catch up before it's too late.*

"Serena wants to keep going!" I yelled out into the night as I resurfaced.

Dad leaned out around the cabin of *The Lady Sea Dragon* and looked past the bow. "The passage is way too shallow for me to get the boat through. I think we're going to have to turn back."

"We don't have any salt left." Cori picked up the salt box and shook it upside down.

"Yeah," Trey continued. "Jade and Serena might be okay, but there's no way Luke will make it back."

"We'll just go see what's on the other side of the passage. One of us can come back and let you know what's over there," I suggested.

"I dunno…" Dad rubbed his head and cringed.

I dove underwater to catch my breath and glanced at Serena. She parted the weedy grass, trying to see through to the other side of the passage. Finalin and Medora might be just on the other side of those weeds, for all we knew. We'd come so far. Having to turn back would break Serena's heart. In fact, from the look on her face, I doubted she would turn back at all.

What do you think? I asked Luke.

I have a feeling she's going with or without us, Luke answered.

"Serena still wants to go. We can't let her go on her own," I called out to Dad.

Dad paused before responding, scanning the passage again. "You'll stick together?"

"Of course," I called out.

"And come right back once you see what's on the other side?" he continued.

"Don't worry!" I replied before diving back in.

"Be careful!" Dad called after me.

The hills along the passage rose on either side of us as we swam toward the open ocean. I imagined the tree-covered cliffs Gran had described from her childhood, but years of clear-cutting by foresters had eroded the cliffs. All that soil had filled in the passage so the water was only a few feet deep, just enough for us to swim through.

Your dad was right, Luke rang. *It's way too shallow for our boat.*

These weeds would probably clog the propellers anyway, I added, trying to relieve my guilt for leaving Dad behind, especially knowing how worried he must be. The weeds swayed with the ebb and flow of the current, and the ever-present bonging noise seemed to keep time with their movements.

At least the water's getting saltier, Serena rang.

Yeah, Luke rang, breathing deeply. *I could get used to this.*

Not too used to it, I hope, I said, studying him. Something was still off with Luke but I couldn't quite figure out what it was. He raced ahead as the moon illuminated our way through the passage. The bottom of the passage started to drop off, and a strong current of cooler water swept toward us.

Awesome, Luke rang, swimming back to take my hand since I was obviously going too slowly for him.

That current feels like it's coming from the ocean, Serena added.

I thought back to the last time I'd been in the Atlantic Ocean off the coast of Port Toulouse. But now we were at least eight miles up the coast. I tried to keep up but Luke was really swimming fast. Like supersonic fast. Faster than I'd ever seen him go.

Slow down! I rang. *You're going to tear my arm off.*

But there was no stopping Luke and Serena once the passage widened, and I could feel the awesomeness of the current and tides wash over my body and tail. We were definitely in the ocean now.

There was no sign of Finalin and Medora, though, and I wasn't psyched about swimming the ocean blue to find two people who'd done nothing but complicate my life.

Hey, guys? I rang. *I told my dad we'd only go to the other end to see if Finalin and Medora were here, then turn back.*

We can't go back. Serena looked at me, a panicked look on her face. *They left the canoe, which means they must have escaped.*

But Serena, I pleaded, *if your mom and dad managed to escape, I'm pretty sure they're long gone by now.*

Not exactly the right thing to say, judging from the look on Serena's face. I swear I put my foot in my mouth more as a mermaid than as a human.

Serena turned out into the vastness of the ocean. *Mother! Father!*

The rush of the water around us made it hard to hear, but there was definitely a response from someone.

Not just one someone—several someones.

Luke and Serena took off in the direction of the rings.

Guys, wait! I called after them. I looked back through the passage. I even popped my head out of the water to see if I could see Dad, Trey, and Cori in the boat, but the channel had been too long and curvy and they were nowhere in sight.

I was stuck all alone, fighting against the crushing current of the open ocean. A knot of panic rose inside my chest.

Wait for me! I rang out, turning from Folly's Passage.

This way! I heard Luke ring back off in the distance. *You're not going to believe this.*

It took a few minutes to reach them against the force of the current. First, I went the wrong way up the coastline, but I stopped when I saw the blinking light of a lighthouse off in the distance and realized I was heading toward a point. Once I got turned around and could make out the source of Serena and Luke's rings, the sound led me to them.

Okay. I grabbed Serena's arm as soon as I caught up. *Let's get this straight. The further we swim from the mouth of the passage, the harder it's going to be to find it again, especially in the middle of the night.*

Look! Luke swam beside us and pointed to a large darkened silhouette about the size of Gran's cottage at the bottom of the ocean.

What the heck is that? I asked.

At first, it just looked like the normal rise and fall of the bottom of the ocean, but soon I could see what Luke saw. The shape of the hull, the long mast sticking up from the mound.

It's a sunken ship, I said in a low ring.

Fortune's Folly, Serena rang.

I thought Gran said the ship sank in the passage. I thought back to the conversation we'd had back in the principal's office on Serena's first day. Cori had later explained how Folly Porthouse had sailed her ship to Europe to go get her fiancé after the Second World War, only to sink the ship while trying to get back into the lake.

It must have gotten swept out to sea with the tides, Luke suggested.

But Gran said divers couldn't ever find this ship, I replied. *Why haven't they been able to see it? We found it after swimming for just a few minutes.*

Listen, Luke replied.

That's when I heard it. The same low ring I'd heard when I discovered Mom in Talisman Lake earlier in the summer. It wasn't like the massive ring from the mer village where the Mermish Council rang supreme, but there were definitely mers down there.

The mer rings must block the signals from the divers' radar. They would never know to look here.

And there's no way any boat is getting close to these cliffs. I could feel the rush of the surf crashing against the cliffs a few dozen feet away. In fact, the ocean was much rougher in this area, far away from the shelter of Toulouse Bay. *But where is the ringing sound coming from?*

Luke pointed to a porthole at the bow of the sunken ship. My heart skipped a beat when I saw a little mer-girl about eight or nine years old. She rubbed her eyes and slipped out of the porthole, smiling as she swam.

An older mermaid about Mom's age reached out of the porthole and grasped the girl's arm before she could get too far. She pulled her back in through the hole and stroked the girl's hair as she studied us from inside the ship.

I turned to Serena and Luke. *Did anyone else know there were mers this far north?*

This is the first I've heard about it, Luke answered.

Hello! Serena called out. *Have you seen two mers go through here? Their names are Finalin and Medora.*

Another face appeared in the porthole. This one was of a man who looked oddly familiar. Could it be Alzear, Reese and Luke's uncle? It sure looked like him. Why would he be this far north? But no. Alzear had been captured and imprisoned in Talisman Lake. The merman and mermaid talked for a moment in low rings, then turned to us.

They were here, the merman called out. *Long enough*

to rest and eat. They told us of their plan to overthrow the Mermish Council and wanted us to join them.

Yes! Serena cried. *That was them.*

What do you know of this plan? the mermaid asked.

Serena quickly explained about the mer revolution and how Tidal Law was forcing Webbed Ones back into the ocean.

Webbed Ones, you say? The mermaid put a hand to her mouth and stared at us.

This has gone on too long, the merman muttered as he placed his hand on the mermaid's shoulder and then looked back toward us. *The Mermish Council must be stopped.*

If you believe that, why didn't you go with my mother and father to help them? Serena asked.

The mermaid stroked her daughter's hair again. The merman drew her close.

We were banished from the mer village when we lost our baby son a long time ago, the merman rang. *The Mermish Council couldn't risk anyone finding out our secret—that our son had become a Webbed One.*

Luke's hand tightened around mine.

We've already lost one child. The mermaid drew her daughter closer. *We can't risk losing another.*

Luke's hand was seriously threatening to crush my finger bones to rubble.

What's the matter? I asked. But then, I looked in the merman's face and saw what Luke saw.

Luke turned to me, his face bright with happiness.

I think I just found my mer family.

Chapter Sixteen

LUKE APPROACHED THE SUNKEN ship as if in a trance. Serena and I trailed behind him at a distance.

Do you really think this could be his family? I asked Serena. Luke had talked about his mer family a lot during the past few months. When his mom got sick and was in the hospital, she'd even told him he could try to find them once he turned fifteen.

Maybe, Serena whispered in my ear as we swam.

As soon as we got close enough to the porthole, though, it was obvious. Bright light from the supermoon shone on the little girl's eyes. They were the same crystal blue as Luke's, framed with impossibly long lashes.

How long ago did your son become a Webbed One? Luke asked the mermaid and merman. *Would he be about my age?*

The mermaid let go of her daughter and swam up to meet Luke. She touched his T-shirt, which looked completely out of place compared to the unclothed mers, then she held her hands out and cupped Luke's face. *Penelopus?* she rang.

At least, it *sounded* like Penelopus, but my Mermish-to-English translation skills were still kind of rusty.

Well, everyone calls me Luke now. Luke blinked a few times and his face broke into a smile. *But, yeah—I think so.*

Luke. The mermaid grasped him and pulled him into a hug. *My son.*

Come, Petra! The merman swept the young mer-girl into his arms, then slipped out of the porthole and swam toward them. *Come meet your brother.*

I have a sister? Luke asked. He looked toward me and made my heart melt with the sweetness in his eyes. Petra reached out and felt Luke's short hair and pulled her hand back in surprise. Compared to their father's long, flowing hair, it looked pretty out of place. Then she reached out again and felt the cotton of his T-shirt.

Hi, Petra. I'm Luke, he said with a quirky smile. *Do you like my shirt?* He pulled it off over his head and offered it to her. *Would you like to wear it?*

Petra nodded and smiled as her mother helped her put the shirt on. They weren't quite sure how to get her arms in the sleeves at first, which reminded me of Serena almost strangling herself with her bathing suit, but after a few minutes, Petra was swimming around showing off her new shirt.

It tickles when I swim! she rang.

The next ten minutes were a flurry of rings as Luke and his mother and father, Pollinia and Portagus, caught up on all that had happened over the past almost fifteen years.

Obviously, they were a family who really liked names starting with the letter P!

Apparently, Luke had washed up onto a beach during a hurricane (which we knew) when he was only about a month old (which we didn't know).

We tried for days to get to you, but the small tidal pool where you were trapped was too far up the beach, his mom, Pollinia, said, stroking Luke's hair.

By the third day, his father, Portagus, added, *a human discovered you with your legs partially formed. The human took you away.*

That must have been Grandpa, Luke whispered to me in a low ring. *What would have happened if he hadn't found me?*

Good thing he did, I replied.

We told the Mermish Council what happened, Pollinia continued. *That's when they sent us away and we were told we could never return. The Dame Council's sister told us secretly of this safe haven.* She waved toward the sunken ship. *It had belonged to her grandmother. When we were driven from the village by the Council sentries, we ended up here. A few years later, Petra was born.*

So the Mermish Council deported you so you wouldn't reveal the secret about Webbed Ones, I said. Just like they were trying to do to Luke during his tribunal.

Not just us. We encountered several other families during our travels.

It was then that I noticed a few more mers peeking out from some of the portholes.

The Mermish Council is so evil, Serena muttered.

Yeah, but—I began. I couldn't help but think I wouldn't have Mom if the Mermish Council hadn't let her be a Webbed One.

No buts! Serena interrupted. *They imprisoned my parents and blamed them for murdering the old Dame Council!*

And threw us in Talisman Lake, too, Luke reminded me.

Okay, okay—I know you're right. We can't keep letting the Mermish Council get away with this crap, I finally said.

Crap? Petra asked as she swam around me and studied my Elmo T-shirt.

Don't teach my sister bad words! Luke laughed. He turned to his mother and father. *Jade wants to fight back. Me, too.*

Me, too! Serena agreed.

Pollinia whispered to Portagus. A dozen or so other mers slipped out of the portholes from the sunken ship and joined the discussion. I didn't catch everything they were saying, but it was obvious Polly and Porty were trying to decide whether they were going to risk joining us.

Okay. We've agreed to join in on the fight, Portagus said.

What about Petra? Pollinia stroked the mer-girl's hair.

Whatever we do, we must face it as a family. The Mermish Council has controlled our lives long enough. Do we have a plan? Portagus asked.

I think our best bet is to figure out a way to get as many mers together as possible, I suggested. *I vote we swim down to Port Toulouse canal and figure out a way to free the Freshies from Talisman Lake and go from there. One of us can stay behind with Petra to keep her safe.*

I had my baby-sitter's course certification if they were looking for volunteers.

That sounds wise, Portagus rang. *We should leave as soon as possible so we can travel under the cover of darkness.*

Hold on a sec. I looked around the water to get my bearings. How far away from the mouth of the channel had we swum? I'd gotten so turned around trying to find Luke and Serena. Then I caught a glimpse of the lighthouse beacon in the distance. *I better let my dad know what's going on.*

I'll go with you, Serena said.

We finally found the mouth of the channel, but the tide had gone out already so there wasn't enough water for us to swim back through. It killed me to think Dad was waiting back there, wondering what was going on.

"Dad!" My face broke the surface of the water and I called out into the night. I tried three or four times before he answered.

"Jade!" I heard his voice call out in the distance. "What's going on?"

"We're all fine! Luke found his birth parents but we can't get back through the channel." I dove back under water to catch my breath.

"Come back!" Dad called after a few minutes.

"I said I can't!" I called again. Meanwhile, Serena pulled at my arm underwater.

We need to go, she urged. *Mother and Father could be miles from here by now.*

With no way to get to Dad and no way to make him understand what was going on, I had no choice. I dove back underwater and joined Serena, Luke, and his mer family as they began the long trek south to attempt to overthrow the Mermish Council once and for all.

It took us at least four hours to swim the eight or so miles from the northern passage of Talisman Lake to the coast off Port Toulouse. The moon was still quite high in the sky and bright enough to light our way. Along the way, we got to know the other mers who had been banished by the Mermish Council.

To our surprise, two of them were Coach Laurena's sister and brother. Luke's mer parents had found them hiding out in a sea cave along the coast after their father died. It didn't take long to convince them to join us once Serena and I told them what had happened to their sister.

The closer we got to Port Toulouse Bay, the louder the bonging sound got. Luke began acting stranger and stranger with each approaching mile.

What's up with Luke? I looked over at Serena, who was still swimming along with Coach Laurena's siblings, but they seemed to have zoned out, too.

Everyone is acting a little strange, Serena replied. She and I didn't seem to be affected by the clanging noise, but something was definitely not quite right.

Hey, Penelopus! I called ahead to Luke. *You okay up there?*

I figured the joke would be enough to get him to knock it off, but he acted like he hadn't heard me. All I could hope was that Tidal Law wasn't still messing with him.

After another hour or so of swimming, I thought we'd be getting closer to the canal, but instead, a huge underground mountain ridge stretched out in front of us.

What the heck? I rang. *Is that the mer village?*

I think so. I don't think we came from this direction last time, though, Serena rang over the thunderous clanging. *And that sound wasn't here, for sure.*

Hold up, everybody! I rang. *I think we took a wrong turn somewhere.*

But Serena was the only mer paying attention to what I was saying. Everyone else swam past us like drones returning to the beehive to wait on their queen. Luke's eyes were glazed over again, and he just brushed past me when I tried to get his attention. A determined scowl creased his forehead as he swam. It definitely wasn't just the saltiness of the ocean water—something else had gotten hold of him.

It's like the noise has hypnotized them or something. How are you feeling? I asked Serena.

I'm totally fine, Serena said.

This way, Portagus said blankly to everyone as he shot off to the base of the stony ridge.

What about the plan? I called out to him. *You know? The Freshies? Strength in numbers and all that?*

And what about the part where I volunteered to stay

behind to look after Petra while everyone else took care of overthrowing the Mermish Council? I thought to myself.

But everyone followed Portagus like a conga line of ants. Left with no choice, I did, too, but I grasped Serena's arm for us to hang back because I couldn't help but feel like we were being led into a spidery web.

My spidey senses must have been tingling, because waiting for us at the base of the ridge were none other than the Mermish Council sentries with long, very pointy-looking spears.

Welcome home, the sentries called out to our group. *Dame Council will be thrilled to hear of your return.*

Like aliens to the mother ship, I rang to Serena, just like Bridget had said.

Only I wished the Smart People had invented space teleportation already, because I would have loved to zap my molecules out of there just then. In fact, I planned to get Dad working on teleportation as soon as I made it back home.

Correction: *If* I ever made it back home.

Chapter Seventeen

I TRIED TO GRAB LUKE and Serena to hightail it out of there, but Luke struggled against me with his freaky blank-eyed stare, and one of the sentries urged us toward an opening at the bottom of the ridge with his spear.

This might actually be good, Serena rang in my ear. *Hopefully they'll lead us straight to Mother and Father. And Bridget, too.*

If you say so. I wasn't quite sure how following a bunch of armed sentries was going to help us overthrow the Mermish Council, but with everyone else in our group acting so weird, I didn't know what else to do.

The clanging noise grew even louder as the sentries led us through a series of caves at the base of the underwater mountain ridge, which opened up into a gigantic valley. And *no wonder* it was so loud—the mountain ridge encircled a giant space several miles wide, and the sound seemed to reverberate against the ridge's walls like a huge amplifier.

The last time I'd been to the mer village, the whole place had been on lockdown because Cori and Trey were in the Martins' boat, *The Lady Sea Dragon*, several hundred feet overhead and everyone had been hidden in their little hidey-holes to make sure they weren't discovered. Little did the mers know that they didn't need to worry since Eddie (our resident mer expert) had figured out that mers gave off a constant ring that blocked boat sonar and radar signals, making them invisible.

This time, though, the mer village was buzzing with activity. Hundreds and hundreds of mers swam from place to place—up, over, and around mossy grottos, swaying seaweed, and barnacle-covered structures—going about their business as the early morning light shone through the water. They cowered and darted away as the sentries escorted us to the middle of the village about a mile or so into the valley.

I managed to swim up alongside Luke as they led us toward an underwater town square. Stalls surrounded the square like at Port Toulouse's farmers' market, but these stalls were stuffed with shellfish and braided seaweed twine and other Mermish merchandise.

Mer-chandise?

Ha! But how could I be making jokes at a time like this? I needed to focus. So did Luke!

Will you snap out of it? I asked, shaking his arm as we swam.

We're here to serve the Mermish Council, Luke said blankly as the bonging rang all around us.

What the heck are you saying? I cupped his face with my hands and turned his head my way to get his attention. *Luke!*

Luke glanced at me and a flash of recognition crossed his face, but it wasn't long before he pushed my hands away, and his eyes glazed over again while the sentries continued to urge our group toward the square.

I spotted Luke's little sister, Petra, at the outer edge of our group.

Mother? Petra tugged on Pollinia's arm, but her mother's dazed gaze was focused straight ahead. *What's happening, Mother? Father?* She swam to her dad, but he was just as spaced out. Petra looked like she was about to burst into tears.

Petra, I rang to her. It wasn't safe for her here. Another reason we should have stuck to the plan! She turned my way, and I waved for her to swim to me and Serena. *It's going to be okay. Come!*

What's wrong with Mother and Father and the others? Petra rang in a worried tone as she stuck close to me while we swam.

We're not sure, but Serena and I are fine, so whatever you do, stay with us okay? I rang.

Petra nodded, and she stayed at the back of the group with us.

They're all under some sort of trance, Serena said, looking from Luke to the others. *I think it has something to do with that clanging noise. Mother told me how all mer-babies are put to sleep to the sound of a bell. Now they're using it to control them, I bet.*

That's like what my mom told me, too! Like Pavlov's dog.

I remembered Dad telling me about the scientist who used a bell to train a dog to know when it was time to eat. *But where would they get a bell?*

That's when I saw a rusted, barnacle-covered ship's bell in the middle of the town square. It was hooked onto a craggy piece of petrified wood and it swung in the swaying water, ringing at regular intervals.

Bong. Bong. Bong.

And why isn't Petra affected? I hugged her close to me and tried to keep her away from the rest of the group. *Or you and me?*

Petra and I weren't born here, Serena said. *Neither were you. I don't ever remember falling asleep to the sound of a bell.*

The sentries motioned for us to wait in an open space in the middle of the town square with a group of other mers. Many, many others were arriving, all sporting the same spaced-out look. I held onto Serena's and Petra's hands, and we worked our way away from the group to the outskirts of the crowd so Petra wouldn't get crushed.

But Mother and Father, Petra rang.

They'll be okay, I whispered. *But I'm not sure what's about to happen, and I know they'd want you to be safe. Just trust me, okay?*

Petra nodded and bit her lower lip just as a thunderous sound filled the air. I turned to see five or six sentries blowing into large conch shells. They accompanied a group of very familiar-looking mers.

It's the Mermish Council, I whispered to Serena and

Petra. The control freaks who'd sentenced Luke, Serena, and me to Talisman Lake to rot in its scum-infested waters with the rest of the Freshies.

The first was a guy I remembered as Jowls, with his thinning hair and sagging, jowly face. He'd been the most vocal of the group, and I was sure he would have preferred to boil us in a fish chowder instead of imprisoning us in the lake. There were others I recognized, too, like the older lady with the seashell necklaces who was the only one who hadn't voted against us.

Leading the pack was Dame Council with her sharp features and cunning eyes. She was accompanied by her ever-present minion. Everyone on the Mermish Council looked bright eyed and non-zombied. Why weren't they being affected by the bell?

Finally, our plan is complete! I heard Dame Council ring as she swam among the group. *Assemble everyone so we can put a stop to this nonsense once and for all.*

I saw Luke make his way through the crowd and present himself to Dame Council.

At your service, Dame Council. Luke swam toward her and bowed his head.

Oh, puh-lease, I muttered from my vantage point across the square. What the heck was Luke doing? Had he forgotten what a jerk Dame Council had been to him last time when she sentenced him to a life of drudgery in Talisman Lake?

*Hmm…*Dame Council surveyed Luke's short hair, but without seeing him with his T-shirt on, she couldn't quite place who he was. She was probably so used to banishing and imprisoning mers that she'd lost track of them all.

I looked down at my own T-shirt and Petra's, too. Thankfully, the mers around us were too spaced out to notice that "one of these things is not like the others," but what if the Mermish Council saw?

We should hide. There was no way I was taking off my shirt just so we could go incognito.

I pulled Serena and Petra toward me and ducked behind a stall in the market so we could watch what was happening without being seen.

Oooh, Serena rang. *Flip-floops!*

I noticed then that the marketplace stall was decorated with sea-worn flip-flops, just like the cart Reese's friend Renata had been pulling when she brought food to the sentries at the tidal pool. I hunted around the stall and there she was, perched behind the counter with her eyes closed.

Renata? I asked but it was no use—she didn't answer. Was everyone under the Mermish Council's control?

A large crowd of spacey-eyed mers was already gathering in the massive square. What the heck were we supposed to do? I tried to focus so I could keep track of where everyone was.

Okay, so my mom and Coach Laurena are in Talisman Lake, and we have me, you, and Luke accounted for. No sign of Bridget yet, but have you seen your mom and dad? I asked Serena.

Serena pointed toward the square and put a hand to her mouth.

A couple of sentries arrived with two mers attached to

stakes like pigs ready for roasting. They were tied and gagged, struggling against the seaweedy-looking twine. Finalin and Medora—prisoners of the Mermish Council.

Wonderful! Yes! Dame Council rang as they were brought to the middle of the square. *Gather, everyone! I have a very important announcement to make.*

Meanwhile, the large iron ship's bell swayed in the current, ringing with the swirling water. The sound filled the village and echoed against the massive canyon's walls. No wonder we could hear the clanging all the way to Port Toulouse.

Soon a crushing crowd of hundreds and hundreds of mers was floating around and above us. At the very middle of the group was Dame Council, flanked by the rest of the Mermish Council and surveying her pod with her sharp eyes. She fiddled with something in her ear and smiled evilly.

What does she have in her ear? I rang to Serena as I held Petra close to me. *It's like she has earplugs or something.*

I might know the answer to that question. I jumped at the voice and turned to see a familiar teenage mer's chubby face and friendly smile.

Reese! I rang over the noise of the gathering crowd. I hadn't seen Reese since we said good-bye at the mouth of the canal leading up to Talisman Lake when the Mermish Council imprisoned us there.

Serena threw her arms around him in an excited hug. It knocked him back through the water, and he braced himself against the market stall to catch his balance. Petra gripped me tightly.

It's okay, Petra, I rang. *Reese is a friend. Actually, Reese is your cousin.*

Reese, this is Luke's sister. Serena took Reese's hand and gripped it tightly to pull him through the water toward us, but Petra turned away and played with one of the flip-flops hanging from Renata's stall.

You like those? Reese rang quietly and reached into his homemade satchel. *Well then, I have something for you.*

He pulled out a colorful girl's flip-flop he'd no doubt scavenged from one of the nearby beaches. Petra took it from him timidly, touched the pink plastic flower, and broke out in a huge grin.

Why can you talk to us like this? I asked. *The rest of these mers are like mindless jellyfish.*

Same reason Dame Council can. Reese pulled his long hair back and pointed to pieces of rubber flip-flop he had stuffed in his ears. *I tried to make some for as many mers as I could, but it's dangerous.*

Renata turned my way. She pulled her hair away to show me her earplugs and winked.

You, too, Renata? Oh, thank goodness. It's the bell, though, isn't it? Serena guessed that. I turned to Reese. *Can you still hear us okay?*

Yes. These just help dull the sound of the bell so we can at least think straight, Reese said.

But how did you know? I asked.

It's easy to make friends when you have something they want. Reese wriggled his eyebrows and made Petra giggle.

That's when I remembered that Reese had been the one to feed Bridget information about what was happening with Tidal Law.

Did you find your mom? I asked.

Bridget, you mean? he asked. That's when I noticed Renata's food cart at his side.

Yes, Bridget, I replied, a hopeful feeling growing in my chest.

Reese pulled back a woven seaweed mat from inside the large cart. Underneath the mat was a large, swollen tail.

O MIGOD, *BRIDGET. ARE YOU okay?* I whispered.

I'm okay, Bridget answered, but the ring of her voice was weak and strained.

She got pulled into the ocean by the tide the other night, Reese rang, covering his mom up again to keep her hidden. *I was able to rescue her and give her earpieces, but I can't do anything for her tail. She really needs to get back to dry land.*

That's when Dame Council began to speak.

You are gathered here today for a very special announcement. Perhaps you have heard rumors about Webbed Ones and such floating around, but I am here to put those rumors to rest. She motioned to Finalin and Medora, who struggled against their bindings. *You may remember these two as the convicted murderers of our valiant past Dame Council. Since they escaped imprisonment, they've been working tirelessly to spread these rumors to divide mer loyalty.*

The other mers from the Mermish Council nodded their heads and added words of agreement, all except the older woman with the seashell necklaces.

Look at that sister of mine, Renata said, waving toward Dame Council.

Who? Dame Council? I asked. *She's your sister?*

Yes, and our grandmother would be ashamed to know how she's lost her way, Renata replied. *Then again—am I any better, sitting here silently?*

Dame Council resumed her speech as I picked my jaw up from the bottom of the ocean floor.

Let me assure you, you have been duped by these criminals and I am here today, standing before you as Dame Council, to finally expose these mers for the traitors they are.

Serena tensed at my side but I held her arm to keep her from doing anything crazy.

Do you understand what I am saying to you? Dame Council nodded her head from mer to mer, as if to make sure the information sank into their brains as the ship's bell kept ringing. *There is no such thing as a Webbed One.*

Yes, Dame Council.

And anyone who continues to defy us by spreading these lies or opposing our laws can expect the same fate as these two. She waved her hand through the water toward Finalin and Medora. *Is that also understood?*

Yes, Dame Council.

This is ridiculous, I rang to Reese.

This has been their plan all along, Reese rang. *Recall all the land-dwelling mers to prove Webbed Ones don't exist and brainwash everyone into following the Council's laws blindly. They'll never let the Webbed Ones return to land.*

Of course! Force all the Webbed Ones back in the ocean, make them forget their human lives, then keep them there to rot so the rest of the mer world would stop believing that being a Webbed One was even a choice. But all of the Webbed Ones I knew didn't actually *have* a choice—they couldn't survive in the ocean. That's why they'd been given land status in the first place!

That's it! I rang. My fear of standing up to the Mermish Council was replaced by a seething rage. *We need to find a way to get Bridget back to dry land and Petra here to safety and then put a stop to the Mermish Council once and for all.*

Oh, and don't forget figuring out a way to give mers a say in what goes on around here, Reese said.

Are you sure we can do all that? Serena asked. *Where do we begin?*

Come on, I replied, grasping the handles of Renata's cart. *If this is going to work, we're gonna need those reinforcements after all.*

Thankfully, nobody questioned Reese with his cartful of goods as he swam through all the spacey-eyed mers listening to Dame Council's one-woman show. It killed me to leave Luke and our new mer friends, and I could tell Serena needed all of her courage to leave her parents tied up at the stake, but we needed a better plan than just rushing the stage.

But how are we supposed to stop Dame Council? Serena rang quietly beside me. Although it was a tight squeeze, Serena, Petra, and I had managed to cram ourselves into the cart with Bridget until Reese could get us across the town square through the mob of mers. *She has everyone under her spell.*

Not everyone, I replied in a low ring. *You, me, and Petra, plus Reese and Bridget, can still think for ourselves. And Renata, too.*

But, it's just the six of us and there are hundreds of them. Serena lifted the edge of our seaweed blanket and scanned the crowd nervously.

It only seems that way, I replied. *Who knows? Dozens more could be in hiding, afraid to disagree with the Council. I have to believe that, given the choice, all those other mers will choose to stand up for what's right. We just need a better offense to make our point.*

Like in underwater hockey, you mean? Serena asked.

Exactly like that, I said, squeezing her hand. *First we need to figure out how to get the Freshies out of Talisman Lake.*

Serena and I slipped out of the cart once we'd emerged from the other side of the tunnels at the base of the ridge and knew the coast was clear. Then we took turns towing the cart with Bridget and Petra still inside.

Oh, hey! I rang to Reese as we swam, pointing to his wrist. *You still have Luke's watch.*

Luke had given Reese his diving watch as a souvenir the last time we'd been in the ocean. Eddie had installed a GPS chip in it to keep track of Luke while he was underwater.

Yes, and it still works. Reese pressed the Indiglo button to make the face of the watch light up.

Cool. One of these days I'll teach you how to actually tell time,

I joked, but I kept checking over my shoulder as we swam away, avoiding any of the well-traveled routes so we wouldn't be discovered. Finally, we arrived at Toulouse Point.

It's a good thing we've been working out for underwater hockey or I might never have made it back to shore, I rang to Serena as I hung on to a huge boulder for a quick rest.

Underwater hockey? Reese asked with a laugh as he checked on his mom.

Is that a game? Petra asked as Serena helped her out of the cart, now that we were safely hidden among the boulders.

Oh, yes, it's a sport I played with the humans when I was up on land, Serena replied.

Speaking of 'on land,' I need to get back out there to find my dad, I rang.

You are Webbed Ones, too? Petra asked, her eyes widening as she glanced from Serena to me. *Mother told me many times that is only a children's story.*

I laughed out loud.

I thought mermaids were only in stories, too, I replied. *In fact, I have a whole series of books about mer-girls just like you.* I remembered my Emily Windsnap books from Gran's cottage.

Books? she asked.

Where we keep our stories, I replied, rearranging the seaweed around Bridget to make her comfortable.

Oh yes. Books and televisions—being on land is so different, Serena added. *They have skateboards and elections and school. Oh, Jade!* she turned to me. *We forgot to turn in our Social Studies project!*

We've been kind of busy, I rang with a laugh. Honestly, we were in danger of being controlled by an underwater dictatorship and she was worried about passing Social Studies?

I know, Serena rang, her eyes downcast. *But it was my first project, and we worked so hard.*

Let's just focus on one crisis at a time. Deal? I asked.

Okay, okay, Serena agreed. *What do you have in mind?*

I need to get my dad down to the shore with the Merlin 3000 for Bridget and find Eddie so he can open the lock. My mind was going a mile a minute, trying to ignore the nagging doubts about everything that *could* go wrong with the plan I was formulating. *But first, I need to find a place for me to sprout legs and get some clothes on.*

I scanned the beach.

My tent, Bridget whispered. She braced a hand against the cart and looked around. *It should be somewhere along the shore if it didn't get washed away. There's a backpack in it with extra clothes.*

Perfect. Reese, you stay with your mom until I can get help down here for you. Serena—can you stay with Petra until the coast is clear?

Yes, of course. But are you sure this is all going to work out okay? Serena asked.

In it to win it, I replied.

It was Friday afternoon by the time I dragged myself up the shore of Port Toulouse Beach. At least I *thought* it was Friday afternoon. Honestly, I was so tired from being up all night, swimming eleven thousand miles, and starving because I couldn't bring myself to eat barnacle slugs and seaweed sandwiches that I didn't care what time or what day it was.

I'd picked the same spot where Luke and I had first met Reese because the point's large boulders shielded me from the public beach. The afternoon air burned my throat as I leaned back against one of the rocks, trying to catch my breath.

I spotted Bridget's tent a little further down the beach. The tent's poles leaned at a weird angle, and a bunch of seaweed clumped around the canvas from the tide. I shut my eyes, willing my tail to hurry up and transform into legs despite the pain that shot through me.

The sun was about two-thirds over me, heading west, so I guessed it was about three o'clock. I tried to focus on the moving clouds to distract myself, then followed the white smoky path of a passing jet high up in the sky, imagining I could just fly out of there and escape. Escape from the pain, from the craziness going on at the bottom of the ocean, from the weirdness between me and Luke about the Fall Folly, and between Cori and me about her mentorship. From myself. My plans. My goals. My doubts.

Escape from everything. Anything. Anything to keep myself from dwelling on the pain in my lungs and legs.

Legs!

I sighed in relief, seeing the goose bumps rise along the skin of my thighs. But my bottom half was barer than a blue jay, so I wasn't exactly ready for prime time. My Elmo T-shirt was baggy but not *that* baggy. I poked my head up and over the boulder to make sure there was no one on the beach, then made a mad dash for Bridget's tent.

The ashes in the campfire had long since been put out and the tent's canvas was dry, probably aired out by the wind and afternoon sun, but Bridget's sleeping bag was still sopping wet. I rifled through a backpack sitting in the corner of the tent. A few protein bars (which I ripped into teeth-first like a hibernating bear), a couple of Band-Aids, a bottle of water, aloe vera cream, a flashlight, ahh…! To my relief, there was an extra set of clothes. Damp clothes, but they'd have to do. Actually, they were pajamas—probably what Bridget had planned to wear on Wednesday night. *If* she'd gotten through Wednesday night.

I found Bridget's sandals underneath the sleeping bag and got dressed quickly, pulling the drawstring of her pajama bottoms to fit me, though the pant legs were about three inches too short.

They would have to do. Her cell phone was there, too, in the front pouch of the backpack. Somehow it had escaped the tide, but there was only one bar when I flashed it on.

"Please work, please work, please work…" I chanted as I stumbled out of the tent, chewing on a protein bar that tasted only mildly better than the insole of a shoe. But the beach's sand dunes and large rocks blocked the cell phone signal. Typical.

I broke into a run along the beach and finally arrived at the wooden boardwalk.

"Three bars. Thank you, Universe." I dialed Dad's number. He picked up on the first ring.

"Hello! Bridget?" he answered. "Are you okay? Are Jade and Micci with you?"

"It's me, Dad."

"Oh, Jade! Thank goodness you're okay! Is Mom with you?"

"No, as far as I know she's still in Talisman Lake," I replied.

"What about the others?" Dad asked.

"They're okay…kinda," I said as I ran along the board-walk, trying to keep the phone at my ear. "Look, it's really hard to explain. Just meet me at the bridge by the canal as soon as you can."

"What do you mean 'it's hard to explain'? Is everyone okay?" he asked.

"Everyone is alive but we need the Merlin 3000 at Port Toulouse Beach for Bridget and we need the Freshies' help to stand a chance against the Mermish Council."

"I'm across town and I'll need to pick up the trailer from home, so it's going to take me at least half an hour to get to you."

"Just hurry! And call Eddie so he can open the boat lock." Maybe I could get Cori and Trey to help, too. Were they in school? Did they even go to school today? "Darn," I muttered under my breath. "What time is it?"

I tried to look on the screen of Bridget's phone but couldn't find the time.

"It's 3:33. Lucky you, you just missed the final bell," Dad joked. "Listen, I'm getting in my car right now, and Eddie and I will do our best to get there by four."

Four o'clock. Mr. Comeau always left school at about four o'clock. Oh, darn, darn, darn! I thought of Serena and our Social Studies project. We had worked *really* hard, and it certainly wouldn't help Serena's case with Principal Reamer if she didn't hand in her very first high-school assignment. Plus, I couldn't really miss handing in any projects, given my track record. Could I make it on time?

"Change of plans," I called into the phone. "Meet me at the school. And please swing by Home Depot for a couple dozen sets of earplugs. Use your frequent buyer points if you have to!"

Chapter Nineteen

I RAN THE WHOLE MILE to the school—up along the canal, across the bridge, and down Main Street. And trust me, for someone with legs that were only five minutes old and sandals two sizes too small, this was no easy task.

A few people coming out of the bank gave me weird looks, but I wasn't sure if that was because I was wearing lipstick pajama bottoms or because Lainey Chamberlain had been busy spreading the word that Serena and I were mermaids. If that was the case, I expected a *National Enquirer* photographer to pop out of the bushes any second. Then again, if Lainey was spreading stories that she'd seen two mer-girls in the community pool, it was equally possible that she was being fitted for a white canvas jacket with wrap-around sleeves that attached in the back. With her mom's sewing skills, she'd be the best-dressed girl on the psych ward.

I should have asked Dad if Lainey's discovery had hit the news when I had the chance, but there was no time to think about it. I yanked open the big blue door to the high school and rushed inside. I could hear Ms. Wilma's office chair's wheels screech across the floor as I hurried down the hall.

"Jade, honey?" Ms. Wilma called out from the office. I knew exactly what she wanted. Well, at least I *hoped* she was looking for Serena's school registration papers and not an autograph from her first ever mer-girl sighting.

"Sorry! Emergency! I really need to use the little girls' room!" I yelled, running past the bulletin board and down a few more hallways before screeching to a stop in front of my locker. I hated to lie, but I didn't have much time and I was left with no other choice. My hands shook as I turned the combination lock to get our Social Studies project. Finally, the lock clicked and I flung the door open.

There was a note on my whiteboard.

I'M SORRY I'VE BEEN SUCH A JERK.
PLEASE COME HOME. –CORI ♥

Along with the note was a beautiful drawing of a girl in a pretty, blue mermaidy dress.

I looked over my shoulder up and down the hallway, hoping to see Cori, but the hall was deserted. Everyone had already cleared out after the last bell. I looked up at the clock on the wall.

3:54.

I had to hurry if I wanted to stand a chance of getting to our Social Studies class before four o'clock.

I rifled through my books and found our project, then shut my locker door and hightailed it to Mr. Comeau's classroom. He wasn't there but, thankfully, his briefcase and keys were still on his desk, which meant he was still in the building. I stashed our project underneath his keys so he wouldn't miss it.

Done!

Serena had better appreciate the fact that I'd run (*run!*) a whole mile to make sure her first high-school project had been turned in on time. I had to admit that it was a relief to me, too, considering I'd scraped by with only a C minus the year before.

"Oh!" I nearly ran over Raymond Fresco on my way out of the classroom. He'd been the other name on the ballot for ninth-grade rep. "I'm so sorry—I really should look where I'm going."

"No, sorry, it was my fault," Raymond said. He had an armful of poster board bundled up under his arm. "I was just pulling down my campaign signs. They're announcing the winners at the dance tomorrow night, but we had to get all the signs down by the end of the day. I noticed Serena wasn't at school so I took hers down, too. I hope she won't mind."

Raymond searched in his bundle and pulled the edge of one of Serena's colorful signs to show me.

"Wow, that was really nice, Raymond." I realized that during all the time we were underwater leading our crazy mer lives, people were walking around doing normal stuff and leading normal lives. At that moment, I wished very much I were more like Raymond Fresco. "Thanks so much."

"Um. You're welcome." Raymond looked at me really strangely. "It, er, wasn't a problem."

I stared back, wondering if he'd heard something about me and Serena. But if Serena's and my secret was out, Raymond would just come out and say it, wouldn't he?

Bridget's phone rang.

"Sorry, Raymond. I really have got to go!"

"So, I guess I'll see you guys at the dance tomorrow night?" Raymond asked. "Tell Serena good luck!"

"Yeah, sure." Oh, yeah—the Fall Folly dance. It was so beyond my thoughts that I'd kind of obliterated it from my mind. "Hope to see you there!"

Raymond waved as I rushed past and answered the phone. "Dad."

"I'm in the back parking lot," Dad replied.

"Be right there."

One of the pamphlets for Mr. Chamberlain's *Safe 2 Swim* program fluttered to the ground as I ran past the information counter outside the pool office. Not seeing Coach Laurena there was so weird. What was happening with her and Mom in Talisman Lake? How had they made it through last night? If luck was on our side, hopefully I would know that before long.

"You made it!" I ran to Dad as soon as I got outside.

"Thank goodness you're okay." Dad grabbed me in a hug and swung me around, then stopped to get a good look at me. He plucked something out of my hair. "Did you know you had a razor clam in your hair?"

"What? Oh." I patted my head to check if I had anything else in there. Fortunately, no.

Is that why Raymond had looked at me so weirdly? Maybe he hadn't been looking at me strangely at all. Maybe I was just going crazy. Gah! I had to get my head together and focus on how to get the Freshies out of Talisman Lake and what exactly we were going to do once we got to the mer village. Wouldn't I be just as useless underwater as I was before, only this time leading a dozen or so more mers to their doom?

It would really help if I could be in two places at once. It was time to call in the fleet.

"Do you have my cell?" I asked Dad, hoping he'd picked it up from Gran's coffee table where I'd left it.

Dad fumbled in his pocket and presented my phone. The battery indicator was red but hopefully it would do.

I scrolled through my contacts.

@geeksrule   Dad

fluke1019   Luke

I found Cori's number and texted her.

hurricanejade: hiiii! am ok but going back under h2o. can u and trey take the boat through the canal?

It took a few seconds for her to answer.

fashiondiva: omgomg! im so glad ur ok!!! how will we know how to find u???

I thought of Luke's diving watch with the GPS chip on Reese's arm.

hurricanejade: tell trey to follow fluke1019. he'll know!
fashiondiva: ok!!! ps did you see mr chamberlain?

The battery indicator flashed.

hurricanejade: um, no? anyway gotta go! l8tr!

Why would I see Mr. Chamberlain? It's not like I'd been sitting in my den channel surfing all day.

"Has there been a press conference or something?" I asked Dad. "Cori said something about seeing Mr. Chamberlain."

"Not that I know of," Dad replied. "I've been checking the news all day and no one has been in touch."

"Well, whatever. Here, can you hold on to this for me?" I handed my phone back to Dad. "And here's Bridget's phone, too."

I spotted Coach Laurena's car in the school parking lot. I remembered how she'd put the underwater hockey equipment in her trunk for our game against Cole Harbor next week. "Just a sec."

Thankfully, we lived in a small town because Laurena's driver-side door was unlocked. I popped her trunk and grabbed the huge equipment bag. If we wanted to stand a chance against those sentries at the other end of the canal, it would help if we were armed.

Eddie arrived in his truck just then and rolled down his window.

"Aren't you a sight for sore eyes! Where are we heading?" he called out.

"To the canal! Got your keys for the lock?" I asked Eddie as I dumped the equipment bag into the back of his truck.

Eddie jiggled the keys in his ignition. "Got 'em right here."

"Excellent!" I got into Dad's car. "What about the earplugs? Oh, and is the Merlin operational?"

"Yes, and yes," Dad replied.

"All right!" I said, slapping the dashboard. "Put the pedal to the metal, Dad."

Dad put the car in gear and peeled out of the school parking lot with Eddie hot on the trailer's bumper.

"But can you swing by Dolly Donuts' drive-through on the way? If I'm going to battle the Mermish Council, two protein bars just ain't gonna cut it."

Chapter Twenty

I SET THE EQUIPMENT BAG down next to the boat lock's control tower. I'd filled Dad and Eddie in on everything that had gone on since the night before—the situation with Luke and his mer family, and the plan to overthrow the Mermish Council, such that it was.

"Okay," I said, wiping the maple glaze from my hands onto my lipstick pajama bottoms.

I unzipped the equipment bag and shook the hockey sticks, fins, masks, and snorkels into the water of the boat lock that separated Talisman Lake from the Atlantic Ocean. "Cori and Trey aren't here with the boat yet, but the sooner we get started, the better. I need Eddie at the controls here to open the lock, and Dad, I need you to get the Merlin 3000 to Port Toulouse Beach to help Bridget."

"Check," Dad said, nodding his head. He handed me a huge Home Depot bag full of earmuff-type ear protectors like the kind policemen used at shooting ranges. "They didn't have the rubber earplugs, but hopefully these will work."

"Well, they're not exactly stealth mode, but they'll have

to do," I joked, dumping the bag into the water with the hockey equipment.

"Are you sure you're going to be okay?" Dad asked. "I almost had a stroke when I lost you last night."

"Don't worry," I assured him. "Mom will be with me this time."

"I guess that's comforting," Dad said, but he looked anything but comforted.

Eddie was in the control tower working the switches. He'd already lowered the gates to raise the bridge, and the ringing bell and flashing lights signaled that it was time for me to go.

"Remember the plan!" I yelled as I cannonballed into the water, but I didn't hear Dad's response over the splash.

By the time the large metal gate from the boat lock opened out into Talisman Lake, I was in full tail mode. Just as I had hoped, Mom, Coach Laurena, and about a dozen or so other mers peeked out from the other side of the gate, welcoming the rush of salty water from the ocean. They all looked pretty zoned out, though, as the sound of the ship's bell continued to reverberate through the water.

Hey, guys! I called out, but everyone ignored me and swam into the holding tank while Eddie closed the lakeside gate. They swam to the ocean-side gate, which was still closed, totally oblivious to the two armed sentries at the end of the canal ready to turn them into fish-kabobs if any of them tried to escape.

I had about five minutes to figure out how to get the

Freshies' attention before the water level in the lock was low enough for Eddie to open the ocean-side gate.

Mom waved her head back and forth, trying to sense the source of the bonging, and I could tell she still wasn't able to see very well. I ripped open the Home Depot bag to hand out ear protectors. There was just a small problem: the bag only had five pairs.

Here guys, put these on. I tried to hand them out to anyone who would take them, but no one paid any attention to me. They were too busy trying to escape to the ocean, guided by the clanging of the bell. I took one pair and forced them onto Mom's ears. It took a few minutes of grappling with her to keep them on before she turned my way.

Leave them on, I rang loudly so she could hear me. *The Mermish Council is controlling everyone with the bell. These will help.*

Oh, Jade, Mom finally said, once she was able to focus on my voice. *Sorry, my eyes still haven't quite gotten back to normal but I'm so happy you're okay.*

I hugged her tightly and tried to fill her in on what was happening while I hunted in the bag for more ear protectors.

Next, I slipped a pair on Coach Laurena and then went from mer to mer to try to decide which mers would get the remaining three. Finalin and Medora's henchmen, for example, could come in handy in the coming showdown with the sentries so they each got a pair. I scanned the rest of the group with my final pair and made my choice.

Uncle Alzear! I cried. Once he had the ear protectors

on for a few minutes and came back to his senses, his face broke into a broad grin.

We meet again!

Am I ever glad to see you! I yelled so he could hear me through the ear protectors. *There isn't much time, but basically, I'm breaking you all out of here so we can make a run on the Mermish Council.*

An excellent idea! he rang.

But we still had a dozen other mers who were really out of it. We needed a way to snap them out of their daze or else they could do more harm than good.

Listen up, everyone! I rang to everyone who could understand me. *At the bottom of the lock, you'll find a bunch of sticks, masks, and equipment. Grab what you can to help the others make earplugs, and when the gate opens, we're going to rush the sentries.*

What about these? One of the henchmen had found the stash of rubber swim caps I'd nabbed from Mr. Chamberlain's booth at the mall. He held up a neon pink one with the *Safe 2 Swim* logo.

Perfect! I said, grabbing another cap floating up toward the surface of the water. Coach Laurena helped me get caps onto five of the mers while the henchman and Mom worked on three others. We stuffed their long tangled hair under the caps and around their ears to muffle the bell's noise. By then, the other henchman had figured out how to rig two face masks over another mer's ears so the eight masks covered four more mers.

You all look great! I beamed. Five mers with ear protectors, eight mers with swim caps, and four with face masks over their ears. We may have looked like a bunch of crazy aquatic clowns who'd just escaped from Sea World, but I only hoped that added to the effect.

The lock's ocean-side gate began to creak open.

Okay, everybody! I continued. *It's showtime!*

Just like we expected, two rather large sentries with long, pointy spears defended the end of the canal. Little did they expect, though, that a bunch of Freshies tricked out in swimming caps, ear protectors, and face masks would be coming at them with underwater hockey sticks.

That alone confused the sentries long enough for Coach Laurena to lead a half dozen or so unarmed mers to the rendezvous at the rocky point. Once the sentries clued in to what we were up to, though, they sprang into action, spears first.

Uncle Alzear and the two henchmen led several other Freshies on offense, cracking hockey sticks against the sentries' spears in a fierce battle while Serena popped out from behind a mossy rock and handed Petra off to Mom. Reese arrived seconds later.

All good? I asked, trying to duck around the fray to let Mom by.

All good, Reese rang back.

You kids be careful! Mom called out as she swam up the canal with her arm draped protectively over Petra, who flinched at the sounds of the battle.

We will, I called out as Serena, Reese, and I tried to join in the fight.

Go, go, go! Alzear called out to me from across the canal as he muscled a spear away from one of the sentries.

We can't just leave you here, I replied, whacking a spear out of the way with my hockey stick.

Let us do our job and you do yours. Go! he roared.

That's when I remembered Coach Laurena's voice. How some of us needed to be on offense and some of us needed to be on defense.

A low rumble filled the water. I looked up the canal and saw the hull of *The Lady Sea Dragon.*

Trey and Cori! That was all I needed to know that we just might stand a chance.

Reese! Serena! Everybody! We're moving out! I yelled to everyone who was free. We zipped over to the rendezvous point to collect the others, then led the charge back to the mer village, *The Lady Sea Dragon* following in our wake.

Chapter Twenty-One

A FUNNY THING HAPPENS WHEN you show up at an underwater mer village with a boat looming overhead. Hundreds of mers scatter like ants in a rainstorm, and the whole place becomes deserted in a matter of seconds. By the time Serena, Reese, and I made it to the town square with the rest of the Freshies, everyone was gone and the ship's bell had disappeared.

I could still hear it, though.

Where's that sound coming from? I turned in all directions.

They took the bell to the Mermish Council Chambers, Renata rang out from behind her stall where she was hiding from the boat. *Dame Council took your friend and a few other prisoners, too.*

My friend Luke? I asked, a familiar sense of dread building in my chest. It was just like the time a few weeks before when Luke had been judged in front of the tribunal. I only hoped they still hadn't figured out who he was.

My sister didn't like the look of him, I guess. Renata peeked out and seemed to recognize a few familiar Freshies in our group, calling them by name. *Oh, Laurena! I saw your brother and sister head toward your family's grotto!*

Coach Laurena brought a hand to her mouth and looked like she was about to burst into tears.

Oh right! I reached over and put an arm around her shoulder and smiled. *I didn't get a chance to tell you.*

There was a rumble from the boat's engine as Trey shifted the boat's gears high overhead. Renata cowered behind her stall once more.

Don't worry about the vessel, Renata. They're our friends. Reese swam to my side. He pointed to the flip-flops hanging from her stall. *But, do you mind if we borrow a few of these? I promise I'll get you new ones once this is over.*

Anything if it means being done with this foolishness. She waved her hand in the air.

Okay, everyone, I addressed the Freshies. *Reese and Laurena will show you how to make earplugs with the flip-flops. Start with your families first and get as many people back to the square as soon as you can.*

What are you going to do? Reese asked as he pulled a few flip-flops from the stall.

Serena and I are going to try to find her parents and Luke, I said. *Renata—do you think you could lead us to the chambers?*

Renata snuck a peek over her shoulder at the hull of *The Lady Sea Dragon.*

Friends, you say?

I thought of Trey and Cori up in the boat—waiting to jump into action whenever I'd need them.

Best friends.

Well then, let's go, Renata replied.

Here, Reese handed me and Serena each a flip-flop, *just in case.*

Thanks, Reese. I gave him a quick hug and he blushed when Serena pecked him on the cheek before we headed out.

We zipped around and through stalls and houses and mounds of kelp and rocks until we reached the outer edge of the village, across the valley from where we'd entered that morning. The area looked vaguely similar to what we'd seen during our Luke rescue mission.

Wasn't there a tunnel around here somewhere? I felt along the bottom of the rocky ridge for where the current swirled and found an opening where the water pushed out at us like the last time. *Oh, here!*

I could hear the sound of the bell pulsing from within the tunnel and was just about to force my way through when Renata stopped me.

No, that's not safe. I used to deliver food here before they took away my privileges. She tugged at my arm. *Come, I know another way in.*

Renata led us a little farther along the ridge through another series of tunnels that converged into the same meeting space where they'd held Luke a few weeks before. This time, we slipped into the grotto from a small opening at the base of the cave while sentries floated by the main entrance above.

The grotto was about as big as the inside of Bridget's

Diner and its walls sparkled with bioluminescence, like I'd seen once on a *Planet Earth* video, lighting the space with a dim glow. We slipped along the far wall, unseen, and settled behind a large pillar of stone decorated with intricate carvings. I poked my head around the pillar to get a look at what was happening.

A lot of familiar faces graced the front of the Council Chambers. There was Dame Council with her narrow nose and sharp eyes, and Jowls with the same jiggly face and ridiculous hair. The nice elderly mermaid with the seashell necklaces was there, too.

Oh, no, I whispered in a low ring. Finalin and Medora were being guarded by sentries. Serena tensed beside me. Luke was with them, too.

I'm telling you, this is the same boy we imprisoned in the lake several weeks ago, Jowls rang as he swam around Luke.

How can you be sure? I was assured he'd been imprisoned with the others. Dame Council studied Luke closely, then turned to another merman, who she pulled by the arm toward her. *And this one—he's not affected by the bell like the others. Who are you?*

As I said, the merman rang, *I'm from another pod across the ocean.*

Nonsense! Dame Council rang. *We are the only pod of mers that exists.*

I couldn't believe what I was seeing at first, but the merman's tanned faced and short graying hair brought me back to that day when a helicopter thundered overhead as we blocked the road leading to the construction site where Mom and Serena were trapped in the tidal pool.

That's Mr. Chamberlain, I rang quietly to Serena as we stayed hidden behind the pillar.

Who? she asked.

Lainey's dad.

Lainey's dad? Serena asked. Her eyes widened.

Everything I thought I knew about the Chamberlains suddenly came into focus. Mrs. Chamberlain had said Mr. Chamberlain had a "rare genetic disorder," which was why they had adopted Lainey. Being a merman definitely qualified as "rare"!

But why would his construction company want to fill in the tidal pool if he was a Webbed One all along? Serena asked.

That's a very good question. Then I remembered. The Chamberlains had moved here from Europe. They weren't even from Port Toulouse. *I don't think he even knew it was there.*

Dame Council and Jowls turned their attention back on Luke.

I'm not sure how he escaped, but he must be sent back to the Freshie prison, Jowls insisted, poking his finger at Luke's chest.

My whole body shook with rage. There was no way I was going to let the Mermish Council mess with Luke again. I had to figure out a way to get the earplugs in his ears so the bell would stop controlling him.

You may want to ramp up security at the lake if you're

planning to put anyone else in there, I said as I tucked the flip-flop under my shirt and slipped out of my hiding place. Serena did the same while Renata stayed hidden.

You! Dame Council swam up to us with the speed of a very hungry barracuda.

Chapter Twenty-Two

*H*OW CAN THIS BE! *How did you escape the lake?* Dame Council stared from me to Serena. She spun around and surveyed the sentries. *Who has breached the lake's security? Who among you would dare? We've already imprisoned Alzear—don't think we will stop at him.*

Alzear is innocent, I rang in an even tone, *just like the rest of the Freshies. Do you think you can just keep locking up everyone who disagrees with you?*

A few sacrificed for the greater good are worth it. Dame Council sneered. *And as soon as we find out how you three got out, we will continue to protect the sanctity of the Mermish Council.*

Haven't you ever heard of free will? Democracy? Serena said in a slow and steady ring. *Power to the people?*

And can you knock it off with the bell? I added. *It's giving me a headache.*

Dame Council checked our ears for earplugs but found none. She swam back to the group and bent her head toward one of her advisors. *Why does she speak to me this way? Why are she and the other one not affected?*

Face it, sister, a voice came from behind. *You can't force everyone to do your bidding.*

Renata slid out from behind the pillar and swam past me toward Dame Council.

Well, thankfully for us, Dame Council spat back as the sisters faced each other, *the bell has been passed on from the original Dame Council Follinia to me and not you, a common servant.*

Renata's graying hair swayed around her angular face. I could see it now—the narrow nose, the intelligent eyes, but on Renata the features looked wise instead of sinister like Dame Council's scowl.

The thing you do not remember, dear sister, Renata rang, *was that our grandmother, Folly Porthouse, was a servant to her people. Something that has become lost on you.*

The original Dame Council Follinia is actually Folly Porthouse? Serena grasped my arm. *With the ship?*

What…? I began.

Grandmother's bell was always meant to serve as a reminder that Webbed Ones, humans, and mers are united. Renata eyed her sister. *It would make her sick to know how you've sullied her memory.*

While Renata and Dame Council kept the rest of the Mermish Council entertained with their squabbling, I drifted over to Luke and plugged his ears with two rubber nubs I'd ripped off the flip-flop.

Shh, I rang quietly, keeping the nubs in Luke's ears as he shook his head back and forth like a horse trying to avoid a buzzing fly.

Serena snuck up behind Mr. Chamberlain on the other side of the room and rang quietly in his ear. He glanced at me, and a flash of recognition crossed his face.

Meanwhile, about a kajillion pieces of the puzzle started arranging themselves in my mind. Folly Porthouse—the woman who sailed the Atlantic to get her fiancé back from the war, only to have her ship sink at the mouth of the northern passage of Talisman Lake. Had she become a mermaid when she "drowned"? But the only way that could have happened was if she'd been a Webbed One to start with. Or was she the daughter of a mer, maybe?

Like me?

Luke was just coming to his senses when the last piece of the puzzle slipped into place in my brain.

Wha…? he rang.

Stay cool, I whispered, grasping his hand as the earplugs blocked the ever-present clang of the bonging bell.

By then, Serena had snuck around the grotto to work on Finalin and Medora.

No matter, Dame Council sneered, still focused on Renata as the rest of the Mermish Council looked on. *You, dear sister, do not get to vote on the matter.*

She may not, but I do, the old mermaid with the seashell necklaces spoke up.

Mother! Dame Council rang in a warning tone. *Need I remind you—you relinquished the bell to me and not her.*

I looked from Renata to Dame Council, then to their mother in the seashell necklace. All of them were related?

And all of them were heirs to Folly Porthouse? This was getting more dramatic than Gran's afternoon soap operas.

And that was a grave mistake, Mother Necklace rang. *I know that now. Especially since I've learned of your murderous plot.*

It had to be done, Dame Council replied. *Control of the Council should never have left our family's hands. And now that I've harnessed the power of the bell, it never will again.*

Your grandmother would not have wanted this, Mother Necklace rang.

Enough! Dame Council rang.

No, the elderly mermaid insisted, her shell necklaces swooshing in the water, *that's not what Folly Porthouse stood for.*

Alert! Alert! Dame Council's minion swam into the grotto. *The vessel overhead has dropped a length of rope attached to a large object into the village. I fear we are under attack!*

The Mermish Council members seemed to lose their minds as they dashed back and forth and in and out of the Council Chambers.

Delegates! Dame Council proclaimed. *Calm yourselves! Please!*

A vessel? Luke finally clicked into what was going on. *Like a boat?*

Trey and Cori, I rang to Luke and signaled for Mr. Chamberlain across the grotto, then Serena and her parents, so they could get set to act.

It sounds like they dropped their anchor, Luke rang.

Yeah, and perfect timing, too, I replied over the mayhem as the Mermish Council members scattered in panic.

Let's go! I rang to Serena, pulling Luke's hand.

Take the bell, Mother Necklace mouthed from the other end of the room.

Serena, Luke, and I swam to the middle of the room to snag the heavy bell, then hightailed it to the tunnel while Mr. Chamberlain untied Finalin and Medora from their stakes.

Renata? I called out, trying to find her in the confusion.

Go, go! Renata called out. One of the sentries had her by the arm, but Mr. Chamberlain, Finalin, and Medora were headed over to help her.

By the time we'd made it through the darkened tunnel back out into the mer village with the bell, Coach Laurena, Reese, and the others had assembled about thirty mers in the square. The Mermish Council must have sent word of what was happening because an army of sentries was heading our way from every direction, despite the looming danger of the boat overhead.

Reese rang out for everyone from his earplugged group to block the sentries. They pulled out sticks and ropes and anything they could find from the surrounding stalls of the market to help arm themselves.

We need to get this bell out of here! I tried to hold the gong so it wouldn't ring but it kept ramming against my knuckles.

Like up to the boat, you mean? Luke asked.

I don't know how we're going to get it up there, Serena

added, repositioning her hands around the bell as it shifted its weight in the current while we swam.

I looked up at the hull of *The Lady Sea Dragon* high above us. Serena was right. There was no way we could swim the bell all the way up there. It was so heavy and awkward; we were barely skimming the bottom of the ocean with it as it was.

But getting the bell out of the hands of the Mermish Council was the only way to make sure they would never again try to control mers with its mesmerizing ring.

To the anchor! I rang to Serena and Luke as I spotted the anchor's line off in the distance.

We swam with all our might toward the anchor about half a mile from the square, but by the time we got there, several sentries had broken free from the scrimmage and were chasing after us.

You guys get it attached! Luke yelled as he swam overhead toward the surface. *I'll let Trey and Cori know to turn on the winch when you give the signal!*

It took a few minutes for Serena and me to hook the iron ring of the bell over one of the prongs of the anchor while Luke swam to the surface. Finally, we muscled it into place and I gave the anchor's line a massive tug. Nothing happened at first.

Come on, come on! I looked over my shoulder at the approaching sentries.

Something whooshed past me.

Watch out! Serena yelled as a sentry's spear nearly missed my head.

I tugged the anchor line again with all my might just as the other sentry took aim with his spear.

Swissshhh…

All of a sudden, the anchor line tightened and I felt myself, Serena, and the bell being snatched from the bottom of the ocean, away from the grasping hands of the Mermish Council's sentries as the winch pulled us up, up, and away.

Chapter Twenty-Three

O NCE THE CLANGING OF the bell finally released its hold on all the mers, the Council members scattered like a school of nervous minnows.

Trey and Cori headed back to Port Toulouse with *The Lady Sea Dragon* to let Dad know to get the Merlin 3000 ready for all the Webbed Ones. Apparently, the tidal pool behind the mall was still too muddy from the construction site for anyone to sprout legs safely. With Mom, Luke, Coach Laurena, and now Mr. Chamberlain in line for the Merlin 3000, it was going to take some time to get everyone back on two feet again.

Once the boat was gone, mers started emerging from their grottos. They gathered in the town square in droves, reuniting with their long-lost Freshie and Webbed One friends and family.

Word spread quickly about the Mermish Council's evil ways, and everyone agreed that the bell of *Fortune's Folly* should be kept up on land so it would never be used against mers again.

Mom! I rang. I spotted her bringing Petra back to her parents, but Petra made a beeline for Luke.

Mom looked my way and smiled. I could tell her eyesight had improved, but she and all the other Webbed Ones were still having trouble breathing.

You did it, kiddo, Mom rang as she swam up to me and pulled me into a hug.

It was kind of a team effort, I replied, looking around at all the happy reunions. Finalin and Medora introduced Serena to some of their long-lost family; Coach Laurena laughed with her brother and sister; and Petra giggled as Luke kept throwing her upward through the water and catching her as she floated back down.

Mom, I asked. *Whatever happened to your family?*

What do you mean? she asked, brushing a floating strand of hair from my face. *You and Dad are my family.*

No, that's not what I mean, I rang. *All the other Freshies and Webbed Ones are meeting up with their families. What about you? Who did you leave behind?*

Nobody. Mom laced her fingers together and shook her head slightly. *Nobody I care to reunite with, anyway.*

I hope that's not entirely true, a voice rang through the crowd. A familiar woman approached, pulling a lunch cart decorated with flip-flops. *Maybe you can find it in your heart to forgive at least one of us for turning our backs on you.*

Tanti Renata? Mom brought a hand to her mouth.

Renata swam to Mom and held out her hand. Mom

took it in hers, and her face crumpled in a look I'd never seen before. Was it regret? Relief?

Nuh-nuh-nuh. Wait just a second, here. I waved my hand in the water, trying to get things straight. *You mean to tell me Renata's your aunt and my great-aunt? Which makes Dame Council my...*

Grandmother? Mom rang, but it wasn't really a question. Mom's face screwed up in a look of distaste. *Yeah. I know—it's bad. I kind of hate to admit she's my mother.*

And my sister, Renata agreed.

No wonder Mom had said Serena could do worse for parents than Finalin and Medora! Mom definitely took the prize in the "dysfunctional family" department.

Well, I turned to Mom, thinking of the mermaid with the seashell necklaces. *At least they're not all completely bad. Plus, that means Folly Porthouse was my...great-great-grandmother?*

Yes! Renata looked up as though doing a mental calculation. *I suppose so! And for that, you can be proud. I know she would have been proud of you!*

Thanks, Renata. I gave her a hug, then corrected myself. *Tanti Renata.*

Will you stay? Renata asked us. *We're preparing a feast.*

Feast? I thought of all the possibilities. Seaweed soup, mackerel sandwiches, eel stew. My eyes must have bugged out of my head because Mom came to my rescue.

Oh no, Mom rang. *I don't think that would be a very good idea. We'll stay for a little while, but it's a long swim back and we really aren't very well-suited to staying underwater for long.*

I understand. Tanti Renata reached out and touched Mom's arm. *But you'll visit sometime?*

Definitely, Mom answered.

That's when I spotted Mr. Chamberlain swimming by himself at the edge of the festivities. For someone who was a "captain of industry" on land, he looked about as out of place as a crab at a lobster convention. I excused myself and swam to him.

Mr. Chamberlain? I rang.

Oh! Jade, is it? His face took on an anxious look, so different from the confident, smug man I first met when he stepped out of his helicopter at our Butterflies vs. Boutiques rally. *I was talking to your friend Luke earlier. He explained everything to me about you and your mother and the tidal pool behind the mall.*

Yeah, about that…

Please… Mr. Chamberlain put his hand up to stop me. *I owe you a huge apology. As you may have surmised, I'm not from around here. I really had no idea you were all mers.*

Likewise! I joked. *Mrs. Chamberlain said you had a "rare genetic disorder," which was why you adopted Lainey, but I never would have guessed* this.

It's not that we didn't want kids of our own, Mr. Chamberlain said. *We just weren't sure what that all would entail, if you'll pardon the expression. Don't misunderstand. We love Lainey with all our hearts, but seeing how you turned out—I guess Mrs. Chamberlain and I needn't have worried.*

I blushed.

Your wife also said you're from Europe. How are you able to travel and everything if you're a mer?

Money can open a lot of doors, Mr. Chamberlain rang. He blinked a few times and a look of regret crossed his face. *It can close a few, too.*

Then something occurred to me. Did Lainey know anything about her dad? *Does anyone else know you're a mer? On land, I mean.*

Well… Mr. Chamberlain drew his chin to his chest. *My wife knows, of course. In fact, she must be beside herself wondering where I am since I never made it home from the office last night before getting drawn into the ocean.*

And Lainey? I asked.

As far as Lainey knows, mermen and mermaids live in Disneyland.

I wouldn't be so sure about that, I began, then explained how Lainey had found Serena and me in the pool after we'd rescued her.

You—you both saved her life, Mr. Chamberlain rang quietly. *Yet another thing for which I'm in your debt. I don't know how to repay you.*

Well, let's just hope your daughter hasn't signed a book deal about what happened at the pool before we make it back to dry land, I joked.

That would certainly complicate matters, wouldn't it? Mr. Chamberlain laughed.

A few other mers came over to introduce themselves,

and soon Mr. Chamberlain was entertaining them with tales of Mermish life across the ocean.

Have you heard? Serena pulled me away from the group, sporting a huge grin after catching up with her parents. *They've captured all the Mermish Council members and Uncle Alzear has been nominated interim Master Council until they can organize a proper election where everyone can vote. Just like at school!*

That's awesome, Serena, I rang. *Who knows, maybe you'll be Dame Council someday. Which reminds me—they're announcing the election results at the Fall Folly dance tomorrow night. Do you think your mom and dad can spare you for the weekend?*

I'll ask, Serena rang, grasping my arm excitedly before she swam away.

The Fall Folly. Right. I spotted Luke and Reese trying to put Renata's stall back in order while Petra attached her pink flip-flop to one of the shelves.

Need some help? I asked, swimming over.

Sure, Reese rang. *I just need to get more of these floop-flops from my grotto. I'll be right back.*

Luke looked up from arranging a pile of twine and smiled his curvy-lipped smile.

Sorry I totally spaced out on you guys, Luke rang. *I'd been so gung-ho to help but ended up making things worse.*

I thought back to how I'd tried to do the same thing by going to talk to Mrs. Chamberlain about Cori's mentorship.

I know the feeling, I said with a laugh. My first order of business when I got back to dry land was to fix things with Cori and maybe get a grip on what I was going to do for my mentorship, too. Surely I had a wider skill set than just bringing down underwater empires. I just hadn't figured out what that was yet.

So, I keep meaning to ask you... I continued. There was another thing I needed to fix. It was now or never. If I didn't ask Luke to go to the Fall Folly dance now, I knew I'd chicken out once we got back on two feet and I remembered what an awkward dancer I was.

Uh-huh? Luke replied. He swept his sister Petra into his arms and nuzzled her neck playfully, then looked back at me with a smile.

Sooo... I said again like an iPod set on "repeat." I stalled for time and turned to Petra. *Did you have a nice talk with my mother?*

Yes! I like her short hair. Yours is long except for this part. Petra reached out and touched my bangs. *Your hair is pretty. Don't you think it's pretty, Luke?*

Very pretty, Luke agreed. He reached out and touched my bangs, too, pushing them away from my face. My heart fluttered like the school of passing fish I caught in the corner of my eye. *Did you want to ask me something?*

Okay. I had just helped overthrow an underwater empire. Surely I could ask a guy out on a date.

Well, remember when I mentioned the Fall Folly dance when we were walking to school last week? I asked.

Yeah. Luke hesitated for a second. *That was weird, right?*

I wasn't exactly sure if you had asked me, then I didn't want to bring it up in case you hadn't—

Oh, I exclaimed. *Because when I told you it was on September nineteenth, not October nineteenth, and you got that weird look on your face, I wasn't sure if you wanted to go.*

And I only got the weird look on my face because October nineteenth is my birthday and I wasn't sure if you knew that, Luke replied.

I stared at him for a full ten seconds before I sorted out all that had happened.

Fluke1019, I murmured. Like the code Trey used to track Luke underwater and the name he used for his cell. October nineteenth. *Your birthday. The day your grandfather found you when you washed up on shore.*

Only, I guess that's not really my birthday, Luke reminded me, *since Pollinia said I was about a month old by then.*

*Which means…*I waited for him to make the mental leap.

*That my actual birthday is somewhere around the nineteenth of September. Wait—*Luke seemed to be adding something in his head—*is that tomorrow?*

Yup, I replied.

I remembered how Luke's mom said he could find his mer family once he turned fifteen, and here he was, surrounded by all of them.

So, I said again. *I was going to ask you to the Fall Folly, but since it's kinda actually your fifteenth birthday tomorrow, why don't you go to the back of the line for the Merlin 3000 and hang out and celebrate with your new family in the meantime?*

Oh yes, oh yes, oh yes! Petra cried.

Well, it seems like one of us likes that idea. Luke laughed and nuzzled Petra's nose, then turned to me. *But are you sure? I'll do my best to get there on time.*

Don't rush. A snort bubble escaped as I laughed. *Trust me, I dance worse than I swim.*

Same here! Luke leaned past Petra and kissed me on the cheek amid the ring of little mer-girl giggles.

Chapter Twenty-Four

"I CAN'T WAIT TO COLLAPSE into my warm, cozy bed," I mumbled, leaning heavily against the passenger-side window as Dad weaved the car through the streets of Port Toulouse late Friday night.

Eddie had the Merlin 3000 all set up at his house along the coast, and he'd started the transformations with Coach Laurena since she was having the hardest time breathing. It would take a while before Laurena, Mom, Serena, Mr. Chamberlain, and Luke all got their turns in the tub, but hopefully Dad's new "upgrades" would speed things up.

"I call it the Merlin 3001," Dad had exclaimed earlier when he told me about the refinements he'd made on the hot tub. "It's got new high-speed jets, titanium valves, and five cup holders."

"Cup holders? Seriously, Dad?" I rolled my eyes at him.

"And an iPod docking station," he replied.

"But is it fast?" I asked.

"What do you think the extra '1' stands for?" he replied with a grin.

I surprised myself—hoping it would be fast enough to get Luke home in time for the Fall Folly dance. But that was kind of ridiculous since I didn't have a dress and I hated to dance. Still, after being underwater far too much in the past few months, "awkward dancing" sounded like the perfect thing for a fourteen-year-old girl—a human girl—to obsess over.

We pulled into our neighborhood, hoping we wouldn't be mobbed by camera crews trying to get the scoop on the two mer-girls discovered at the local pool, but the streets were eerily quiet. When Dad turned onto our street, though, we were greeted by the same black sedan that had met us there a few weeks before.

From what I could see by the light of the streetlight, the car held Mr. Chamberlain's two enforcers, the one with the glasses and the other one with the moustache. Last time we'd run into them, they were hot on our tails trying to get evidence away from me to save Mr. Chamberlain's construction project. Why were they back?

"It's those guys again." I nudged Dad and pointed. "They work for Lainey's dad."

"I called Mrs. Chamberlain to tell her about her husband earlier. What could they want?" Dad asked.

"Did Mrs. Chamberlain say anything about Lainey? Did she tell Lainey about her dad? Did Lainey say anything about *us*?" I asked.

"Honestly, it was a quick phone call," Dad said, rubbing his hair with one hand as he steered with the other. "I had to call Daniel to let him know where to meet Laurena, then call Bridget to see how she was doing, and then there were Luke's parents—"

"What if Lainey *still* doesn't know?" It had been over twenty-four hours since Lainey Chamberlain had confronted us on the pool deck and discovered our mer secret. A lot could have been going through her scheming little brain since then. "What if she put these guys up to this and they've got a news reporter in the backseat or something?"

"Let's just play it cool," Dad said as he gripped the steering wheel to drive around them.

Dad parked the car in our driveway and we got out. I snuck a peek back down the street, but it was too dark to see anything.

"Maybe it's just a slow day for corporate takeovers," I joked, trying not to freak out as the motion sensor turned on our porch light and we climbed the front steps to our house.

Dad fumbled for his keys, dropping them to the ground in the process.

"Here, let me," I offered, picking up the keys so I could unlock the front door, but I could see the car's headlights turn on out of the corner of my eye. "Oh, no. Dad, they're coming down the street...they're at the end of our driveway right now..."

One of the tinted windows rolled down halfway to reveal a passenger in the backseat.

"We're fine." Dad sighed in relief. "It's just Mrs. Chamberlain."

"*Mademoiselle* Jade?" she called out to me. "*Voilà!*"

"Why does she want me?" I whispered to Dad, but he looked just as confused as I was.

Mrs. Chamberlain leaned out the window and held out a box. Dad and I walked to the end of the driveway together.

"What's this?" I asked, taking the box in my hands.

"*Une surprise*," Mrs. Chamberlain said with a wink. "Open it once you get inside so you can see it properly."

I looked past Mrs. Chamberlain into the darkened car. Lainey was there, her eyes wet and swollen.

"Lainey." I hugged the box to my chest. "Are you okay?"

Lainey nodded but said nothing more.

"We have been discussing Lainey's father," Mrs. Chamberlain said quietly, "and you and the other girl, of course. It's all still new right now but we shall see our way through. Isn't that right, *chérie*?"

Mrs. Chamberlain took Lainey's hand and squeezed it. Lainey looked at her mom and smiled, then laid her head against her mother's shoulder.

"Well, we must go," Mrs. Chamberlain said quietly. "You must rest after your ordeal."

"Thank you, Mrs. Chamberlain," my dad held out his hand to shake Mrs. Chamberlain's, "for coming by and setting our minds at ease. You don't know how much it means to us to know our secret is safe with you."

"And likewise," Mrs. Chamberlain said, patting Dad's hand.

"Yeah and, um, thanks for this, too, by the way— whatever it is." I held up the box.

"Oh, it is not from me. I just put the finishing touch." She signaled for her driver to go.

"Wait. What?" I asked as the car pulled away.

"Call *Mademoiselle* Cori," Mrs. Chamberlain said as she raised the tinted window. "She will tell you the rest."

I stood at the bottom of the driveway with Dad, trying to piece together what had just happened. Lainey hadn't blabbed about Serena and me, other than to her mother. And she wouldn't. Not now—not ever—considering her dad had the same secret.

Was life actually going to get back on track? For real this time? It had to.

We were safe. And home.

And famished.

"You hungry?" I asked.

"Starving." Dad put an arm around me and we headed up the driveway. "Let's order pizza."

It was nice to know some things never changed.

I'd called Cori and she insisted on coming over before I opened the package.

She looked like she was about to jiggle off the couch as I pulled the coral blue dress from the *Boutique Chambre Laine* box. It was the same color as the tankini I'd bought with her at Hyde's Department Store four months before. The one with the *Michaela* tag that had reminded me so much of Mom.

"What on earth?" I stood and pulled the dress toward me and looked down.

"Do you like it?" Cori asked in an excited voice.

"I…I love it." I'd never been a dress-up kind of girl, but the fabric, the color, the details were all so amazing that I couldn't help but gasp. Plus, the dress looked about my size. I looked up at Cori. "Is this for me?"

"Of course it's for you, you dope!" Cori said.

"But how did you—did you *make* this? When did you have time?"

"Well, it's not like I whipped it up last night. I've been working on it for quite a while," Cori replied.

Dad came from the kitchen with the pizzas that had just arrived. He placed them on the coffee table with our sodas. I hung the dress's hanger high along the living room's curtain rod for safekeeping while I grabbed a piece of pizza, but I couldn't tear my eyes away.

"Your mom gave me your bathing suit and a few pieces of clothes so I could get the fit right," Cori said as she took a slurp of soda.

"Did you know about this?" I eyed Dad.

"Maybe," Dad said with a sly smile as he munched on his pizza and clicked on the TV.

"No wonder I couldn't find my tankini for underwater hockey! That was cruel and unusual punishment, you know, making me go back to the mall for a new bathing suit." I whacked Cori in the arm.

"Yeah, sorry about that," Cori said with a laugh, holding up her soda so it wouldn't spill and wiping her mouth, "but it was the only way I could pull it off without you knowing.

I wasn't sure how the dress would turn out, and I kept waiting for you to *finally* ask Luke before showing you."

"But I was too chicken," I said sheepishly, pulling a string of cheese from my pizza slice.

"Then, I messed up the zipper, which almost ruined the dress," Cori continued, "and I started to really doubt whether I was cut out to be a fashion designer. When you told me you'd talked to Mrs. Chamberlain for me…I guess I kind of freaked out."

"Yeah, sorry for going behind your back like that," I said.

"I'm the one who's sorry. I guess my pride got in the way. But after you disappeared, it felt like if I didn't finish the dress, it would mean you weren't coming home."

"But how did you have time?" I asked.

"Well, it was just the zipper, so I sucked it up and called Mrs. Chamberlain," Cori admitted. "Plus, I wanted to find out whether Lainey had said anything about you and Serena. By then, Lainey had spilled her guts to her mom about you guys, and Mrs. Chamberlain was freaking out about her husband, so I filled in a few holes about Tidal Law."

"That's why you asked me if I'd seen Mr. Chamberlain in that text!" I exclaimed. "I thought you meant he was in the news or something!"

"Oh, sorry!" Cori said with a laugh. "Well, anyway, Mrs. Chamberlain and Lainey and I had a good talk about everything, and Mrs. Chamberlain offered to fix the zipper in time for the Fall Folly. Which is tomorrow night, remember?"

Remember? I'd been obsessing about finding the right

dress for the past two weeks. And then there it was, just like in a surreal Cinderella moment, only the field mice and birds hadn't sewed and mended my dress. Cori had. Like the true friend she was.

"But, I might not actually have a date, remember? He's at the bottom of the ocean."

"Well, Serena won't have a date either, but I can share," Cori said. "Trey will be our date. Oh, and he finally got his driver's license—maybe he can drive!"

"No, no, no-no…" Dad said, putting down his pizza and wiping his face with a napkin. "Three young ladies in the same car with a brand-new driver? I don't think so. I'll drive!"

"So, it's settled then?" Cori asked, grabbing a piece of pizza for herself.

I stared at the dress hanging from the curtain rod, lit up by the living-room lamp. It sparkled like the ocean in the moonlight. I couldn't believe I owned something so beautiful. But what about shoes? I doubted my tattered sneakers would be a good look.

"You don't happen to have a pair of glass slippers to go along with this dress, do you?"

"Got that covered, too." Cori put down her pizza and wiped her hands on her jeans. She pulled three pairs of silver flip-flops from a bag she'd brought with her, each of them hand-decorated with seashells and plastic flowers. "Flip-floops!"

"They're perfect," I said.

Maybe I could do this Fall Folly thing after all.

Chapter Twenty-Five

"I BET I'M THE ONLY guy here with *three* dates plus a brand-new driver's license." Trey smiled broadly as Serena, Cori, and I walked arm-in-arm with him into Port Toulouse Regional High's Fall Folly dance on Saturday night.

"It's a *learner's permit*, not a driver's license—big difference, by the way," Cori said. Trey had obviously neglected to mention that teeny bit of information. "It's lucky Jade's dad drove us so we didn't have to skateboard over here."

"Details, details," Trey joked.

Cori had loaned Serena a funky, ankle-length dress from her collection, and our *Cori Originals* swooshed over our bedazzled flip-flops as we entered the gym. We'd all gotten ready at my house once Mom finally made it back home and helped us do our hair. Mom even convinced me to wear a little makeup.

"Should be fun!" I said with as much conviction as I could muster while seeing everyone else paired off in couples in the darkened gym, dancing, chatting in corners, or sitting at tables.

"Should be *awesome*," Cori agreed just as Trey made a beeline for his friends at the snack table. "And…we lost our date. So awesome."

"Oh, pretty!" Serena marveled as the DJ turned on the colorful stage lights. The disco ball hanging from the rafters sent sparkles of color dancing along the gym walls.

Serena walked to the middle of the gym floor and twirled in place, mesmerized by the colors, her long golden brown curls swaying around her.

"I can't believe she might get kicked out of school on Monday," Cori said as we grabbed a few seats at an empty table.

"I know," I replied, thinking of Principal Reamer's deadline. "I've kind of gotten used to her."

"I think a few more people might be disappointed to see her go," Cori said.

A couple of guys had walked up to Serena and asked her to dance over the loud music, but from what I could tell, she didn't notice any of them.

"Ah! I can't think about that right now. Not tonight, after everything we've been through. Let's just enjoy ourselves in our awesome dresses." I smoothed the fabric of my dress as I sat down. "Thanks again, by the way. It really is perfect."

"Well, I may not be an underwater mythical creature but I do know my way around a sewing machine," Cori whispered. "And a seam ripper."

"So, does this mean you'll be doing your mentorship with Mrs. Chamberlain after all?" I asked.

"As a matter of fact, yes!" Cori replied.

"Oh, good," I gripped her arm and gave it a squeeze, "because I was so mad at Lainey for not telling you to call her mom."

"Yeah, about that…" The look on Cori's face was confusing. She was smiling but she also looked a little embarrassed. "Lainey actually *did* tell me Mrs. Chamberlain wanted me to call but—"

"But what?" I asked. Cori shifted uncomfortably in her seat. "Spill!"

"Well, I kind of blew Lainey off."

"You what?" I cried. "Why would you do that?"

"She'd just been so mean to you. Then all the stuff that happened this summer—"

"And you thought it would help the cause if you gave up your mentorship? You dope!" I laughed. "This is your dream, Cori. I wouldn't want you to do anything to ruin that."

"Okay, okay," Cori replied with a smile. "I get it. I actually apologized to Lainey and sorted things out with her mom so it's all good, but what about you? Did you decide what you're going to do for your mentorship?"

"Not yet." I spotted Coach Laurena chaperoning the dance with a few other teachers on the other side of the gym. "But I'm working on something."

"Cool," Cori said as she stood up. "I'm gonna go find Trey to get some drinks. Are we good?"

"We're good," I replied as she headed for the refreshment table.

Suddenly, I felt a shift in the crowd. One by one, people turned just as Lainey Chamberlain entered the gym. She looked beautiful in a pale yellow, off-the-shoulder dress with a chiffon skirt. Her hair was swept into an updo, and her bangs were flat-ironed to the side in a sleek, sophisticated style. Her eyes sparkled and she smiled in a way I'd never seen her smile before.

And on her arm was Mr. Chamberlain—looking dapper in a suit and tie, much like I'd remembered him from before. This time, though, his face was relaxed and smiling.

Lainey spotted us. She seemed to hesitate, but then she stood on tippy-toes and whispered something in her father's ear. He nodded and followed her as she headed our way.

"Hello," Lainey said as she approached. Cori looked at me warily from the refreshment table on the other side of the gym, and Serena drifted back to my side from the middle of the dance floor.

"Um, hi, Lainey." We hadn't really had a chance to talk since our quick chat through the car window the night before. "You brought a date? It's good to see you up and around again, Mr. Chamberlain."

That meant Lainey's dad, Coach Laurena, Serena, Mom, and Bridget had all made it through the Merlin 3001, but there was still no sign of Luke.

"Oh, I can't stay," Mr. Chamberlain said. He motioned to the stage where his two aides were helping to mount the bell from *Fortune's Folly* next to the speaker's podium.

"We got it all cleaned up to donate to the school like your mother requested. I wanted to come by with my men to install it. And to give you this."

He pulled a yellow business envelope from under his arm. He was about to hand it to me but then noticed Serena. "Actually, this should go to you. I emailed a copy to Jade's dad, but I thought you'd like one, too."

"Thank you." Serena took the envelope but didn't seem to quite know what to do with it.

"Open it," I whispered.

"Oh!" Serena ripped open the envelope. She pulled out a couple of official-looking documents and handed me the envelope so she could inspect them.

"They're school records…" I said slowly as I read over Serena's shoulder while she flipped through the pages, "for you, Serena!"

"For me?" Serena's eyes widened.

"It even has a letter of recommendation from an actual principal," Lainey added as she pointed to one of the papers.

"Lainey thought that would make it seem more official." Mr. Chamberlain smiled at his daughter.

"How did you do this?" I asked, not believing what we were seeing.

"Eddie put me in touch with his sister in Australia," Mr. Chamberlain said. "She connected me with a charity that does remote learning via Internet to some of the smaller South Pacific islands. I made a sizable donation to their cause and, well—"

"It means you can stay at our school," Lainey said to Serena. "Officially this time."

"Wow!" I wasn't sure what had me more speechless— the fact that the whole "school registration" nightmare was over or that Lainey Chamberlain actually had a hand in making it happen. "I really don't know what to say. This is going to change everything."

"Well, not everything," Mr. Chamberlain replied. "I'm still working on passports for everyone, but that will have to wait until I get back to the office on Monday." Mr. Chamberlain put his arm around Lainey's shoulder. "Until then, I was thinking of taking the rest of the weekend off."

Passports? That would mean Laurena and Daniel could actually get married, and Mom and Dad, too.

"Thank you so much, Mr. Chamberlain," I said breathlessly.

I only wish I could do more, he rang to me. *You and your family have given me my life back. And saving Lainey from drowning like you did? If there's anything else I can do—*

Well. Actually, I might have a teensy favor to ask, I replied. I caught Coach Laurena's eye across the gym and waved, and she waved back with a big smile. All of a sudden my mentorship plan seemed crystal clear.

"I was wondering if I could help Coach Laurena with your *Safe 2 Swim* program for my ninth-grade mentorship," I said.

"I couldn't think of a better candidate. Send the paperwork to my office," Mr. Chamberlain said with a wink as he kissed Lainey good-bye and headed for the door. "On Monday!"

Just then the music stopped and the screech of the microphone filled the air. The regular gym lights were turned on, blinding us with their fluorescent white glare.

"Awrraah..." A groan rippled through the crowd.

"Test, test...Can everyone hear me?" Principal Reamer called out from the gym stage as everyone quieted to hear what she had to say. "Welcome to the Fall Folly, every-one. A time when we celebrate strength of character and bold choices—while being supervised by a twenty-to-one student-to-adult ratio, so don't get any funny ideas."

She nodded to the parent and teacher chaperones stationed strategically around the gym floor.

"We have a few announcements," the principal continued. "First, we'd like to thank the Baxter Family for donating the bell from the ship *Fortune's Folly*. It truly is magnificent and will be enjoyed by generations to come."

There was a round of applause. Trey actually whistled from the other side of the gym as he and Cori walked our way.

"Now," Principal Reamer continued, "it's time to declare the winners of the recent school elections."

"Serena," I whispered and nodded to the stage. Serena slipped the papers back into the envelope and placed it on the table, then took my hand. By then, Cori and Trey had arrived with drinks from the refreshment table.

"Election?" Serena whispered in my ear.

"Yeah. Hey, you pronounced it right." I nudged her shoulder and smiled.

The principal ran through the results for School Council president, vice president, secretary, and treasurer.

"And now for the individual grade representatives." Principal Reamer turned over her paper.

I squeezed Serena's hand and caught a glimpse of Lainey standing alone near our table.

"Hey, Lainey," I called to her in a loud whisper and offered her my other hand. She shrugged and let out a little laugh, then took my hand.

"And our new ninth-grade representative position goes to…"

Chapter Twenty-Six

T HE GYM WENT SILENT and a few people looked our way. The election battle between Lainey and Serena hadn't been a silent one and I'd been caught smack-dab in the middle of it, so people were probably wondering why all three of us were holding hands like Girl Scouts kumbaya-ing around a campfire.

Principal Reamer cleared her throat before announcing the winner.

"Raymond Fresco!"

I actually laughed, hearing Raymond's name. Like that loud, snorty, wild-eyed laugh I excelled at so much.

Trey and Cori looked at me like I was a crazy person.

"Come on, you gotta admit. That's hilarious!" I said breathlessly as I tried to calm my laughter. But it was too late. I cackled like a ticklish hyena and tears streamed down my cheeks, probably destroying whatever makeup Mom had managed to get on my face.

"Raymond did have nice signs," Serena said with a giggle. "Even if they were not pink-screened."

Lainey laughed out loud.

"See? Even Lainey thinks it's funny." I turned to Trey and Cori, but they were already laughing, too.

"Sorry you guys lost, though," I said to Serena and Lainey. "I know you both worked really hard."

"Oh, well." Lainey raised her hands in defeat. "I guess it was time for me to retire anyway."

"Also, thanks." I lowered my voice to a whisper while Principal Reamer continued reading the results from the other grades. "For, you know, Serena, and for keeping our secret." Lainey had only just found out about her dad the night before. She could have done a lot of damage spilling our mer secret in the meantime. But she hadn't.

"The thing is..." Lainey said, looking around to make sure no one was listening. "When I saw you guys in the pool like that—and then your mom—a lot of things started to make sense. Cori explained why you'd worked so hard to shut down my father's construction site to save your mom. And then when I found out about *my* dad—"

"I'm sure that freaked you out, huh?" I asked.

"Yeah. And...well, I guess you could say I saw you in a whole new way once I understood you a little bit more."

I thought about that for a second. It was true. From Lainey's point of view, I probably seemed as mean to her as I thought she was being to me. I'd avoided her like the plague, trying to keep my mer identity a secret; I ruined her father's big construction project; and I'd let my feelings get in the way of the school election. How many of my problems with Lainey had I brought on myself?

And as far as Lainey was concerned, how much of the way she acted came from being misunderstood? Ignored? "I have to say, I think I understand you more now, too, Lainey. That can only be a good thing, right?"

"Definitely," Lainey said with a smile. Then, a familiar mischievous expression puckered her lip-glossed lips. "Now, if you'll excuse me—my date totally bailed on me so I think I'll go see if Raymond Fresco has a girlfriend."

Lainey headed over to his table.

"Yo, dudes!" Trey sat hunched over his phone and waved his hand to get our attention over the music that had just restarted.

"Dudes?" Cori yelled. "You show up here with three gorgeous dates on your arm, then ditch us for the snack table and call us *dudes*? Really romantic."

"Sorry, but Luke just texted me to tell me he's on his way over!" Trey replied.

My heart rate tripled at the mention of Luke's name. My phone buzzed, too.

fluke1019: heard trey stole my date

hurricanejade: get here soon b4 cori clobbers him LOL

fluke1019: poor trey. i guess i got all the smooth moves in the family

hurricanejade: haha…he could use some brotherly chips

hurricanejade: lobsterly tips

hurricanejade: lobsterly lips!!

Gah! How did "brotherly tips" become "lobsterly lips"? I stopped before autocorrect got me into even more trouble. There was a very long, very painful pause before my phone buzzed again.

fluke1019: }O< ♥ <--fisherly lips ok?

"I couldn't figure out how to do a lobster." I turned just as Luke reached our table.

"Luke!" I didn't care how it looked. I jumped from my seat and bear-hugged him in my flip-flops and fancy dress. He wrapped his arms around me and picked me up off the floor and swung me around. Just once, which was impressive since I probably outweighed him, so I appreciated the effort.

"I'm sorry I'm late," Luke whispered in my ear. "We had a slight delay."

"What kind of delay?" I asked. But that's when I spotted him. "Oh! Serena…"

But Serena's eyes were already glued to the big double doors where Luke had just entered. Standing in the doorway was a familiar, round-faced teenage guy, holding a box.

"Reese," Serena said, springing from her chair.

Reese's mom, Bridget, was with him. She waved to me and whispered something in Reese's ear. He smiled and held out his arms for Serena as she ran toward him.

"That is *so* awesome," I whispered to Luke.

It was almost comical seeing Serena and Reese together,

now both of them with legs, because Reese was about three inches shorter than Serena, even in her flip-flops. But she didn't seem to mind.

Reese caught Serena in his arms while a few guys who had asked Serena to dance looked over and shook their heads, wondering who the new dude with the scraggly long hair was. Unsteady as he was on his new feet, Reese stumbled back and they both ended up in a heap on the floor, laughing.

Serena grabbed Reese's hand and pulled him up. He turned to wave good-bye to Bridget before walking to our table.

Mother tells me I should never show up for a date empty-handed, Reese rang.

He placed a box on our table and opened it. Inside were three wrist corsages.

"Aww, that is *so* sweet!" Cori cried, then turned to Trey. "See? Corsages—that's romantic. Mental note for next time, okay?"

"Who do you think ordered them?" Trey said as he placed a corsage on Cori's wrist.

"Really?" Cori asked, her eyes shining with happiness. "You did?"

"Of course," Trey said sweetly, then kissed her.

Did you? I mouthed as he looked over her shoulder while they hugged.

No. He mouthed back, bringing a finger to his lips.

I put a hand to my mouth to stifle a laugh.

For you. Reese placed a corsage on Serena's wrist and kissed her hand.

"And you." Luke slipped mine on. *I didn't buy them, either.*

"I don't care. I'm just so, so happy you're here," I whispered.

Luke brought a hand to my cheek and looked at me for a long time. "I'd rather be here than anywhere else in the world."

I thought about our human and mer worlds and how much life had expanded over the past few months. We'd both gained whole new families.

"Sorry I broke up your reunion, though." I suddenly felt really bad, considering how much Petra adored him. "You really didn't have to rush back."

Though I was glad he had.

"And miss awkward dancing in the middle of our high-school gym with you?" Luke led me onto the dance floor and spun me once before pulling me close into a slow dance.

"Wow. It's almost like you planned that," I said, amazed that we'd managed to pull off a semi-respectable dance move.

"Maybe I did." Luke's face was so close to mine that our noses almost touched. The small scar over his eyebrow where I'd maimed him with my braces back in fifth grade looked faded and almost invisible.

"Luke Martin?" I asked, thinking of Folly Porthouse sailing her ship across the Atlantic to retrieve her fiancé at the end of the war. Surely, if she could do that, I could do what I was gearing up the courage to do.

"Yes?" he replied, his breath warm and sweet on my face.

It was time for me to make a bold move. "May I kiss you?"

"Well, that depends." Luke's eyes crinkled at their

corners. "Are you okay with having a boyfriend who visits his mer parents on alternate weekends?"

"That sounds like the best of both worlds to me," I replied, then kissed him.

As our lips touched, Luke pulled me close, and our last few months together swirled through my mind.

The first time I bumped into him at Dooley's Drugstore. Kissing him at Cori's pool party when I found out he was a mer, too. Losing him to the ocean after he'd helped me rescue Mom from the tidal pool. How he'd played his guitar for me on Port Toulouse Beach.

We'd been through so much both on land and at sea.

"Ouch!" I cried as Luke stepped on my flip-flopped foot.

"Sorry!" he replied. "I told you I wasn't much of a dancer."

"Maybe you should stick to skateboarding," I suggested with a smile.

"Now you're asking for it!" Luke warned.

I laughed as Luke twirled me around and around, making me dizzy and giggly as the colorful lights swirled all around us.

Did I have the best of both worlds, too, I wondered, as Luke caught me mid-twirl and pulled me close again.

I rested my head on his shoulder as we slow-danced in the middle of the gym floor. I glanced from Cori, touching the petals of her wrist corsage while Trey held her hand, to Lainey dancing around Raymond Fresco, then to Reese and Serena doing a weird mer-dance next to our table while a few people looked at them like they were from outer space.

I really *did* have the best of both worlds. The very best.

"Hey, Luke?"

"Yeah?" he replied, looking into my eyes.

You wanna go show Reese a few awkward dance moves on those new legs of his?

"Let's do it!" Luke squeezed my hand as we headed off the dance floor to drag Reese and Serena and Cori and Trey back along with us.

I was starting to understand this whole "girl power" thing, after all. Folly Porthouse didn't just wait around for stuff to happen. She *made* things happen.

Was I anything like her? Was I brave? Was I fair? Was I kind?

Maybe I didn't have things totally figured out yet—like how to be friends with girls like Lainey Chamberlain or how to be somebody's girlfriend when I barely knew the first thing about dating.

But spinning and dancing and funky-chickening in the dizzying colorful lights of my high-school gym— surrounded by friends who were brave and fair and kind—I hoped Great-Great-Grandma Folly would have approved.

Luke's Five-Minute Peanut Butter Cup S'mores

HI, GUYS! I KNOW more about skateboarding and guitars than I do about cooking, but I roast a mean marshmallow and hope you'll try these s'mores (in honor of my buddy Reese) at your next campfire.

Ingredients
- Marshmallows
- Reese's Peanut Butter Cups
- Graham crackers

Campfire Method
1. Roast the marshmallow until golden brown.
2. Place a peanut-butter cup on a graham cracker, then the marshmallow, then another graham cracker.
3. Wait a minute until the peanut-butter cup gets gooey.
4. Eat it.

See? I told you I wasn't much of a cook.

If you don't have a campfire, don't worry. You can do this in the microwave, too.

Microwave Method
1. Place a graham cracker on a microwave-safe plate.
2. Place a marshmallow on top of the graham cracker.
3. Microwave for 10 to 15 seconds. The marshmallow will puff up and melt.
4. Take it out of the microwave, add a peanut-butter cup, and top it off with another graham cracker.
5. Wait a minute until the peanut-butter cup gets gooey.
6. Eat it.

At least both methods end up with you *eating* it.

Enjoy!

—Luke

Acknowledgments

Writing a book is a lot like playing underwater hockey without a snorkel, but it is a process made much easier with a winning team of critique pals, friends, and family.

Many thanks to my agent, Lauren MacLeod, who drafted me from her slush pile and who always makes me feel like I have a "one-man advantage." Thanks also to my editor, Aubrey Poole, for her fancy stick handling and for helping me get the puck to the net.

Marcelle, Charlotte, and Gord: you are my winning hat trick and my constant sources of support and inspiration. None of this happens without you.

About the Author

Hélène Boudreau never spotted a real mermaid while growing up on an island surrounded by the Atlantic Ocean, but she believes mermaids are just as plausible as giant squids, flying fish, or electric eels. She now writes fiction and nonfiction for kids from her landlocked home in Ontario, Canada. Her first book of this series, *Real Mermaids Don't Wear Toe Rings*, was a 2011 finalist for the Society of Children's Book Writers and Illustrators' Crystal Kite Award.

You can visit her at www.heleneboudreau.com.